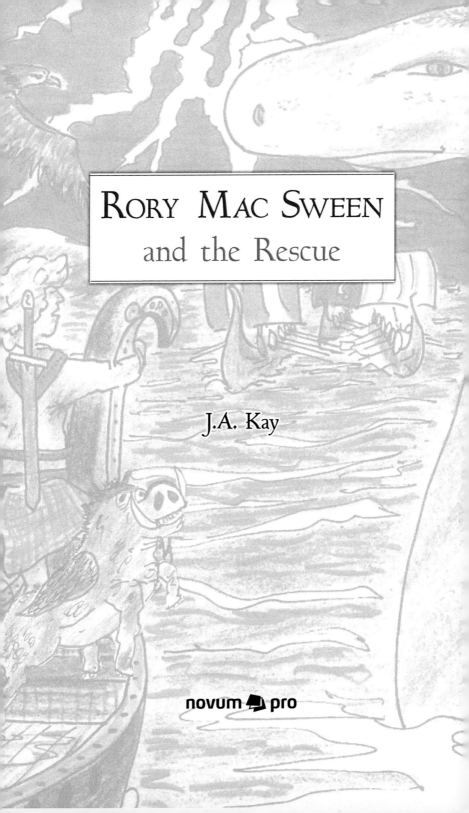

RORY MAC SWEEN
and the Rescue

J.A. Kay

novum pro

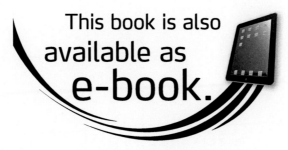

This book is also
available as
e-book.

www.novum-publishing.co.uk

© 2019 novum publishing

ISBN 978-3-99064-518-5
Editing: Hugo Chandler, BA
Cover photos: J.A. Kay
Cover design, layout & typesetting: novum publishing
Internal illustrations: J.A. Kay

www.novum-publishing.co.uk

Contents

About the Author

J.A. KAY was born in 1960 and was raised on the west coast of Scotland where he completed secondary education at Greenwood Academy in Dreghorn. He was fortunate to have William MacIlvanney, the Scottish Novelist and short story writer and poet, as his English teacher in the 1970s. His success inspired him to put his own stories to paper. Other notable pupils who were educated at this Academy during this time included the actress Julie Graham, the singer and songwriter Eddi Reader and the First Minister of Scotland Nicola Sturgeon.

The author served as a Police Constable for thirty years in Scotland and he decided to write as a hobby, on his retirement. His interests include Masonry, Rugby, Martial Arts, Real Ale, and spending time with his two adult children and two granddaughters, and not necessarily in that order. With these life experiences providing valuable background information and the Ale acting as a catalyst for his imagination, these stories were developed.

He has travelled extensively in Scotland and abroad, and he has been aware of the cultural and the mythical stories of the creatures from the Highlands of Scotland since childhood.

He visited Loch Ness both as a child and as an adult, where the stories of the Monster and the Wild Haggis were implanted in his mind. He became aware of the history of the Druids and the power of the Lay Lines when serving in Kilwinning where the Police Office is adjacent to the ancient Abbey and No. 0, which is debated to be the first Masonic Lodge in Scotland if not the world.

He learned at this time that all the Lay Lines passed through both Stonehenge and the Kilwinning Abbey, and he witnessed their power seeping out, affecting the local area when a piece of masonry fell from the Abbey through the roof of a colleague's car after he raised his fist and voiced his disbelief in the magic contained within the building.

It is from this background of dealing with and experiencing emotional and sometimes traumatic life experiences, balanced by black humour that this story unfolds.

Thanks

Special thanks to my patient wife Ann who has travelled this adventure through life with me, and who had a few unique holiday experiences on research purposes along the way.

Also, to Bill Petherick for his artwork, designing the book covers for the novels, making them so special.

In addition, I would like to thank my family for their support and for their encouragement throughout this process, and you the reader, without whom the inspiration to write them would not have been possible.

Final thanks are reserved especially for my granddaughters, who are a couple of lovable wee wild Haggis.

Preface

Rory Mac Sween had believed that his father was dead and that his Mum Mary would never be happy. She was married now to his Stepdad John Grant, who owned Urquhart Castle on the banks of Loch Ness. He was a drunken, violent and abusive man full of his own self-importance and unnatural urges. He bullied everyone, as he could from his privileged position, and he targeted those who disagreed with him, especially Rory's Mum.

Rory had the chance to change this and to protect himself and his Mum when he found the Hagpipe giving him the abilities of the Haggis, which included increasing his strength, speed and intelligence, and it gave him the ability to travel the Lay Lines through time from the connected point, and the Portal hidden below the castle.

But he had lost the Hagpipe and was just an ordinary boy again with no additional powers and he could not enter the time shift caves or call on his animal friends Hag, his pet wild Haggis, Nessie the Loch Ness Monster, and Ben the Giant Scottish Eagle, to assist him.

Saint Columba had a book detailing the premonitions of the future of Rory's life and they had told him that his father was alive and that he would save him. How was this going to be possible, as unknown forces were lining up against him to prevent the fulfilment of this prophesy?

Before he did anything, he had to remake the Magic Sword he had recovered from the Druids millennia in the past. It contained the opposite tusk of the Hagpipe and possessed great power, to be used for either good or evil!

Rory's greatest enemy was time. The Spey-wife had foretold that he could not reclaim the Hagpipe until eight years had passed. Everything was against him, but he had to find a way as the clock was running down, with his Dad struggling to stay alive, a prisoner of the Vikings trapped in the past. Only with the remade Sword and the Hagpipe combined would he be ready to face the Vikings and rescue his Father.

But would he be eight years too late?

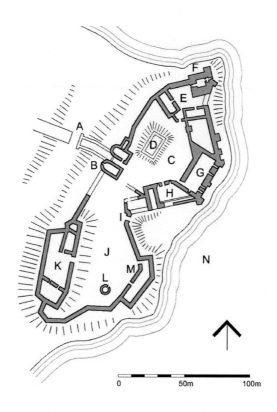

Key: **A** Drawbridge **B** Gatehouse **C** Nether Bailey or Outer Close **D** Temple **E** Inner Close/Monastery/ Refectory/ Schoolhouse **F** Grant Tower **G** Great Hall **H** Kitchen/ Residence Spey-Wife **I** Water Gate **J** Service Close **K** Stables and Shell Keep **L** Doocot/Home Carrier Pigeons **M** Smithy/Brewery/ Distillery **N** Loch Ness

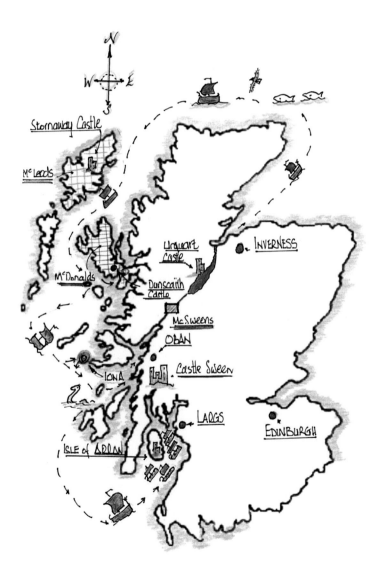

CHAPTER 1

Confidences

Rory was devastated. How could he rescue his Dad now, he felt weak and his skin was soft again, he was just an ordinary boy. He had searched all around the pool cave but the Hagpipe was gone.

Tears streamed from his eyes as he remembered the warning from Granny Grant to look after the Hagpipe and to never lose it. Eight years of hardship would face him if this happened, she had said. He left the pool cave and stepped onto the beach and he walked with an almost broken heart to Hag's cave where the mound of ivory tusks of the Haggis Graveyard should be.

There was no shimmering curtain of time shift power at the entrance. He stepped into the cave which was illuminated by the reflective crystals in the roof and walls, but the cave was empty. No sign of the Haggis Graveyard or the circular rock nest where his pet Haggis Hag was born, or any sign that that she had even been here.

The only living thing in the cave were rats, loads of them scurrying about the sandy ground and up and down the access tunnels to the mountain and the castle buildings above. They squeezed through cracks in the tunnels into the castle store rooms, in search of food, of which there was a plentiful supply, but not for long, going by the number of them.

The tunnels used to be connected to the portals, enabling the dying Haggis to make their final journey to the Haggis Graveyard. Now they were only good for vermin to infest the castle. Without his pet Haggis to control them the castle would soon be overrun with rats and disease ridden rather quickly.

Rory felt distraught. He had lost everything! He kicked out at the rats at his feet who thought that he was a cheap meal. Rory was devastated, and he felt that he had no hope or future, what was he going to do?

He could hardly see through the tears that flooded from his eyes as he stumbled out of the cave onto the beach and right into the arms of the Abbot who embraced Rory warmly, letting him cry himself out. A large white cotton handkerchief was produced from inside the Abbot's brown habit which he gave to Rory to wipe away his tears and the snot. Rory babbled about everything that had happened, to the Abbot. he would know what to do, he had the book[1].

Rory thought to himself as he tried to control his emotions, he understood now. He could confide in the Abbot and tell him all he knew about Saint Columba. He had said that he was going to save his Dad and then he had to go and see him at the Abbey in Iona. Saint Columba was fully aware of Rory's future and Abbot MacCallum had his book. All that Rory knew was that he was helpless

---

1 The Book of Saint Columba showing the records of his Premonitions detailing Rory's life.

without his animal friends and the power of the Hagpipe. He did not understand how he could fulfil these premonitions.

"I've lost the Hagpipe," he cried out to the Abbot as more tears streamed down his face.

The Abbot consoled Rory, giving him a cuddle. He spoke quietly telling him that losing the Hagpipe was pre-ordained for a reason, and that time and circumstances would restore it to him. They would work together studying the book of Saint Columba, and he informed Rory that he would now have to work very hard to be ready for the time when he would recover the Hagpipe and his power.

Rory understood that he had no advantages just now, and that he would have to rely on his own abilities.

The Abbot said, "I will now start work on a gift to help you, but you have to remake the sword first"[2].

Rory could not think straight, how could anything but the Hagpipe help him? He racked his now slow brain, questioning himself. How could the Abbot help him? Rory had concealed the sword from him, but the Abbot knew about it!

The answers to all his questions must be in the book!

But how could he fix the sword? He was just a wee boy and a trainee blacksmith just now. He only had the strength and the knowledge to make nails.

---

2 Broken magical Sword recovered from the Druids in Book 1 Rory Mac Sween and the Secrets of Urquhart Castle.

The Abbot saw the questioning look on Rory's face and he told him, "This is going to take time and hard work, but you will get all the help that you need."

Rory knew what time meant. Eight years before, that was what Granny Grant the castle Spey-Wife had said. Well he would just have to knuckle down and get on with it!

The Abbot placed a comforting arm around Rory's shoulders as they both walked towards the spiral staircases which lead upwards to the temple above in Urquhart Castle. The Abbot explained to Rory that it was going to be a very tough predictable life of hard work, without the uncertainty and the thrill of adventure, and the power brought by the Hagpipe. Rory was painfully aware of this as he felt his soft skin and his sluggish mental ability, which seemed as if he was thinking inside a bowl of thick porridge, and not in super-fast speed like before. He did not like being normal and unable to benefit from the Hagpipe's enhancements, with only himself and his own abilities to rely on.

Rory had counted on its power to travel to the past to save his Dad. He was stranded there, a slave of the Vikings for another eight years, due to his carelessness.

Could his father survive as their prisoner for that long?

CHAPTER 2

The Lost Dad

Ruaidri Mac Sween (Suibhne) grew up in the ancient Sween Castle in Knapdale in Argyll, Scotland. He was the first born of the sixth generation of the Mac Sween Clan to inherit the Hagpipe from his father on his eighth birthday. On this day his father Aodh Ruadh (Red Aidan) relinquished the power of the Haggis which was transferred to Ruaidri, enhancing his natural abilities.

The Clan Mac Sween had grown very powerful thanks to the Hagpipe. They controlled land and power from Lochranza Castle on the Isle of Arran to Loch Awe in the North of the mainland, and Loch Fyne in the south. Their influence stretched all the way to Ayrshire and the estate of the powerful Earl of Montgomerie, where the Monks of Saint Columba were planning a new Abbey at Kilwinning. The Monks had their power base on the Isle of Iona, where all the early Clan chiefs were inaugurated and buried with their blessing.

The Clan Mac Sween had prospered so much that they had expanded into Ireland, controlling Doe Castle in County Donegal and large parts of Munster and Derry, where the Clan split, becoming Mac Sweeney and used other names like MacQueen. A descendant of this offshoot called Steven was transported generations later, across the Atlantic to the Americas. A later male child of his blood line called Steve would become famous for a Great Escape after a motor cycle stunt in a movie.

If only Ruaidri could escape!

All was not rosy in Scotland over this six-generation period which endured the first great War of Independence, followed by a civil war. Clan Mac Sween lost most of their power in Scotland and they had to retire to their lands in Ireland to survive, following major losses in battle to the English controlled armies of Sir John Menteith[3].

Ruaidri was a young man when he buried his father Aodh Ruadh (Red Aidan) in Derry, Ireland following his death fighting to hold onto his land from the descendant of Sir John Menteith known as Sir John the junior.

It was at this time when Ruaidri met and married the beautiful Mary (Maire) O'Neill who was a descended from the Milesian Kings of Ireland, and whose roots were traceable back to the family of Noah and his Ark. They had a son Rory who was the seventh generation of Mac Sween's. Unknown to Rory, he was the culmination of all the previous generations of Mac Sween's and he had inherited all their skills and gifts.

This was the happiest time of Ruaidri's life and he decided that he would take his new family home to Sween Castle and free it of English rule, and the control of the

---

3 Tradition has it that Menteith betrayed Sir William Wallace to English soldiers in the battle of Independence, which led to Wallace's capture and torturous execution (see film Braveheart) and his later nickname Fause Menteith ("Menteith the treacherous, false." Excerpt from Wikipedia.

descendants of the treacherous Menteith's. He would use the Hagpipe and with its aid secure the castle for his son Rory to inherit his birthright.

Unfortunately, on arrival in Inverness at the winter equinox, Laird John Grant was at the docks on business. He saw Mary with Ruaidri and young Rory and he was captivated by the beauty of Mary. He was used to getting what he wanted and he wanted her!

He was filled with an unquenchable craving for her, and he decided there and then that she was going to be his at all costs. The fact that she was taken only made his desire for her stronger.

John Grant contracted a press gang of thugs loitering at the docks, to ambush Ruaidri and put him on a ship to America. He thought of a devious plan to rescue Mary when she was at her lowest ebb with no hope and in despair at the loss of her husband. He would be her saviour and worm his way into her affections and make her his.

This almost went fully according to his plan as Ruaidri and his family had left Inverness on route to a traveller's inn he knew, where he was going to spend the winter months and then travel to Sween Castle. They were passing the extensive standing stones of Clava Cairns[4] which were adjacent to the road, when the ambushers pounced!

Ruaidri told Mary to hide and she quickly grabbed young Rory and concealed themselves in the bracken at

---

4 Historic Scotland Site consisting of groups of stone circles and are the remains of a temple between two huge Cairn burial vaults.

the side of the road, telling him to keep quiet. Ruaidri ran from the ambushers with his rucksack and his possessions, which he was sure the bandits were after, not realising their true purpose. He fumbled with his rucksack trying to get to the Hagpipe in its box to give him the strength of the Haggis to fight off his assailants.

He dodged in and out of the tall standing stones in the circle in an attempt to lose his pursuers. The setting winter sun hung low in the sky, sending a low beam into the entrance of the North East Cairn, illuminating its middle and catching Ruaidri in its spotlight as he was surrounded by the thugs with nowhere to go.

Unfortunately, or fortunately for Ruaidri, he took hold of the Hagpipe box as the ruffians armed with large cudgels (Wooden Clubs) converged on him. He was forced back into the passageway to the entrance of the Cairn. The portal on the lay line network did not need much coaxing to activate as the trapped sunlight within the Cairn burst out of the chamber drawn to the presence of the Hagpipe.

Ruaidri was bathed in the blinding bright light at this winter equinox on the twenty first of December. As he touched the Hagpipe the light shimmered around him and Ruaidri fell backwards into it, vanishing falling through a crack in time. The rucksack containing the Hagpipe still in its box fell forward, landing outside the Cairn, leaving it in the present. The superstitious thugs surrounding Ruaidri saw him disappear and they took to their heels, not wanting to face the same fate in the beam of light that shone out the empty Cairn entrance.

They ran for their lives from the stone circle and probably are still running.

John Grant was watching from a short distance away and he could not believe his luck at Ruaidri's unexplainable disappearance. He was aware of the mystic occult past and history of Scotland, and had sought the services of a witch before, who had predicted his rise to power at Urquhart Castle. He knew of the magical powers at work at the summer and winter equinox, and he still kept the good luck crystal charm that the witch had given him concealed on his person. It was obviously still working as he laughed to himself, but he too was wary of approaching the Cairn to recover Ruaidri's rucksack. The witch's crystal was vibrating below his shirt, and he could see the entrance of the Cairn shimmering in front of him.

He crawled on the ground like the rat that he was reaching for the rucksack, pulling it towards him away from the Cairn. The shimmering stopped as if a switch had been thrown as he crawled away from the cairn. John Grant was oblivious as to why it stopped. It was because the power of the Hagpipe had been removed from its close proximity to the Cairn. He concealed the rucksack behind a standing stone on the outer circle and regained his horse. The Constable of the keep, the giant ex-soldier John Gregg, was waiting at the wagon train of supplies, which had been procured at Inverness when John Grant rode up to him.

The Constable was unaware of his master's devious plot and had remained with the convoy of supplies, as his master left, on the pretence of riding ahead to attend to a call of nature. On John Grant's return he loudly ordered the Constable and his men to search for Mary's husband in a false show of aid, and concern for her and young Rory. He knew that there was no way that they would find him, and he had to suppress his enjoyment, as he accompanied the Constable in the search, leaving the wagon's drivers with Mary and Rory to protect them and to guard the cargo. He made sure that part of the search included the area where he had concealed the rucksack which he recovered with much commotion, ordering an extensive search of the surrounding ground.

They returned after a thorough search and John Grant, with a sad face, instructed the Constable to break the news of the negative result of the search for Ruaidri to his wife Mary. The only thing that had been found was the rucksack which John Grant gave to Mary with fake sorrow in his eyes. She identified it as her husbands, which proved his disappearance if not his demise. Mary was distraught, and John Grant easily convinced her to come into his care and protection, backed by the honest report from John Gregg the Constable, of the genuine search that he and his men had carried out.

John Grant took Mary to the nearby Travellers' Inn, where she had been heading with her husband and their son, to celebrate their first Christmas in Scotland together. John Grant put on a great act as the perfect honourable gentleman and he generously paid for the whole party to spend the night at the Inn. The next morning, he left his contact details with the Innkeeper in front of Mary. Should Ruaidri make enquiry there looking for her, he would know where to find her. Mary had no other option now; she was in a strange country without any friends. She very reluctantly agreed to leave with John Grant and Rory to a life without her husband, and a miserable first Christmas at Urquhart Castle.

Ruaidri fell through time, due to the unpredictable effect of the lay lines aligning with the winter equinox and the random activation of the Hagpipe. He appeared in thirteenth century Norway in 1250 AD, in the reign of the Norse King Haakon IV (Haakon Haakonsson).

The King, unfortunately for Ruaidri, was camping at the standing stones of Nesje on his way to the town of Molde. Ruaidri had nowhere to hide as he had practically appeared in the middle of their camp in his highland dress. He was quickly taken prisoner as a Scottish spy, and enslaved by the Vikings and put to work rowing their long boats.

Ruaidri was used to travelling through the standing stones with the Hagpipe when he was younger, but he was trapped in the past without it. He resolved himself to put all his efforts into surviving as he faced a life of hard labour, beatings, poor food and the cold.

He had to find a way to get back to his wife Mary and wee Rory who needed him. Only his size, strength and determination to get home gave him the will to fight for his life. He also wanted revenge and he had a picture in his head that filled him with anger and inspired him, giving a boost of energy when he needed it.

It was of a wee (small), dark haired, rat faced man who he saw telling the thugs to get him!

CHAPTER 3

Doo's and Horses

So much had happened in such a short time since Rory's eighth Birthday. The Scottish summer sun was still shining as he emerged from the temple with the Abbot. The first thing that he had to do was go see Granny Grant the Spey-Wife, and he let her know what was happening. As he walked up to her cabin he heard a voice that he recognised inside the closed door, his Mum!

He stood outside listening, as he heard Granny say to her, "This medicine will stop you conceiving another child and if he asks, tell him it is for the pain from the beatings that he's been giving you".

Mum was still being hit by his stepdad Rory thought, and he would have to ask Pooie Doo (The nickname for Father Doogan who taught natural science, due to being covered in pigeon poo from his care of them) what conceive meant. If only he still had the Hagpipe he would beat his stepdad and let him know what it was like to suffer!

Rory heard his Mum push her chair back to get up to leave. He quickly stepped back from the door, pretending that he was just walking up to it as they came out. His Mum and Granny were both very pleased to see him, with his Mum giving him a warm welcome and big kisses and cuddles. After a few minutes his Mum said that she would have to go, and Rory saw her put a small pouch in her pocket.

Granny went to her fire and warmed up some of her special Haggis for him. Rory ate it, which made him feel a lot better and he told Granny what had happened, and all about the Abbot and the book. Granny nodded, and she told him he would have to come and see her every day from now on, as he would need her special Haggis to stay strong. Rory promised, and then he went to look for Angus, the oldest apprentice at the blacksmiths, to see if he could get a martial arts fighting lesson from him.

He felt that he would need to know it, now that he could no longer call on the power of the Hagpipe.

Monday came, and Rory settled into a routine of work at the forge, before school, learning how to beat iron and do minor repairs to farm implements and general goods and then back for more work afterwards.

He studied very hard and he was determined to learn as much as possible to prepare him for whatever might be ahead. He watched and learned from Hamish and the other blacksmiths. They were impressed with his commitment and enthusiasm, and they were glad to teach such a willing student. Every spare second of the day was given to his education, with very little time given to play and relaxation. As a result, his body and his mind were being toned in ways that he was unaware of.

As promised he continued with his special lessons with the Abbot and accompanied Pooie Doo (Father Doogan), to the Doocot where he learned how to train the pigeons to return to their own coops, and to carry messages folded in fine soft waterproof lead bands, attached to their legs. The pigeons arrived in wicker baskets periodically by cart and boat from other Abbeys and Monasteries of the Monks of Saint Columba, where they returned when they were released.

This was a very sophisticated messaging system. The "pigeon post" may have been a little slow but it usually arrived. If the distance was too great for one pigeon to fly, then the message was transferred to another one at the closest Abbey to its final destination and sent on its way, until it arrived at its journey's end. This way, information and credit note transactions from the issuing Abbeys were updated and the receipts were returned by cart, along with each new batch of pigeons. Only then were the transactions finalised in the accounts of the issuing monastery.

Information was very valuable, and the Monks were constantly being updated on items of importance from everywhere where they were situated, which was in all the major cities and places of importance. The Monks awareness of current events made them a major influence in the control of the country. This was the first truly workable messaging system and some unscrupulous landowners knew the value of the messages carried by the small birds. They would supply their tenants with nets fixed to long poles, to intercept the birds as they flew past, with a reward for each message retrieved, and a free pigeon pie for supper.

The tenants called this the inter-doo-net which was very similar to today's internet, but it was far more secure than the modern version, as they rarely succeeded in intercepting the messages. As anyone who has ever tried to grab a pigeon stealing crumbs from their feet will know, they are very hard to catch!

Rory was amazed at the complexity of the system with all the cages named with the destination of the pigeons, from the Abbey in Iona to the monastery in Kilwinning and all the places in between. Only the pigeons from Urquhart Castle were allowed to fly free, as they were already home and they wouldn't fly away. The rest were kept segregated and were only released outside when they were flying home with their message attached.

During this first instruction from Father Doogan, Rory took the opportunity to ask him what conceive meant. Father Doogan went a bright scarlet colour, and began stammering about this subject being for a later lesson in biology when Rory was older. This confused Rory and he pressed the matter, looking for an answer. Father Doogan eventually relented and asked Rory if he had seen the ram with the sheep in the fields. Rory answered he had and Father Doogan with a sigh of relief explained that was how the lambs in spring were made or conceived. Rory disliked his stepdad even more now for doing that to his Mum, but he understood what Granny Grant was doing with her special medicine, saving his Mum from giving his stepdad another child.

Johnny, his young stepbrother, was spoiled rotten and he was starting to behave just like his father, treating his Mum like a servant, trying to order her about.

Not having another Johnny would be a good thing!

Rory thanked Father Doogan and hurried off to the stables where a riding lesson had been arranged for the boys of the castle of his age, from Murdo Hands the head stableman. All the boys and wee Charlie Campbell were already lined up in the paddock at the side of the stables when he arrived.

Each one stood next to a horse suited to him, picked by measuring the size of the horse in comparison to the number of Murdo's hands joined together. This system is still used today with horses measured in HANDS! Rory saw wee Charlie standing next to a small pony of three hands, which was smaller than the paddock fences. Its saddle was on.

Murdo saw Rory arrive and he shouted to him to go into the stables and pick a horse. He already had a favourite, a young jet-black stallion who he had been visiting giving him crab apples since he was born two years before. He called him Jet and he had responded to the name, so the name stuck. As soon as he saw Rory he started throwing his mane back and neighing, in anticipation of a treat.

'Just as well he had lifted a few carrots from the kitchen earlier,' thought Rory, as he held one out on his open palm. Jet gobbled it down, greens and all, and began nudging Rory with his nose around his plaid, looking for more.

He petted Jet and he told him "later," which he accepted and stood still as Rory put on his saddle, bit and reigns. Jet walked out calmly beside Rory to the paddock where the other boys weren't having the same success. Murdo Hands was shouting at some of them as they chased loose horses about the paddock, and others were getting into a right pickle, trying to put saddles on.

He saw Rory with Jet all ready, and standing calmly, and he smiled at him, and asked him to give the other boys a hand. After a short period of time, Rory's carrot supply was exhausted, but order was restored.

Wee Charlie looked pleased with himself as he had managed to put the saddle on his pony all by himself, and he climbed up the fence and onto the pony. As a reward, Murdo said that he could go first. Wee Charlie's big smile soon changed to a squeal, as soon as he started to move. The whole saddle spun round, dangling him upside down below the pony, with Charlie still clinging on, looking through the front legs of the horse, as it walked round the paddock.

Everyone burst out laughing. Even Murdo had tears running down his face as Charlie screamed for help. Well, so much for that lesson, but everyone else made sure that their saddles were tight!

CHAPTER 4

Halloween

Time passed rapidly as summer gave way to autumn, and the start of winter, with all the children of the castle and Castletoun getting excited with the arrival of Halloween on the thirty first of October, when they blackened their faces to ward off evil spirits and dressed up to go out "guising"[5]. All the children of the castle and more especially the ones from Castletoun were very excited at the prospect of receiving a special treat, that they were not used to getting.

Mrs Paterson the head cook had been busy organising all her staff by preparing special treats for the hoard of small visitors she was expecting as soon as it got dark, and for the feast in the Great Hall for all visiting dignitaries coming to celebrate All Hallows at a fancy-dress ball.

---

5 Halloween, or Hallowe'en a contraction of All Hallows' Evening, also known as Allhalloween, All Hallows' Eve, or All Saints' Eve, is a celebration observed in a number of countries on the thirty first of October, the eve of the Western Christian feast of All Hallows' Day where masquerades in disguise carrying lanterns made out of scooped out turnips, visit homes to be rewarded with cakes, biscuits, sweets, fruit and sometimes money. If children approached the door of a house, they were given offerings of food. The children's practice of "guising", going from door to door in costumes for food or coins, is a traditional Halloween custom in Scotland. These days, children who knock on their neighbour's doors still have to sing a song or tell a story, to receive their similar reward.

The weather had been kind for the time of year, although it was getting a bit cold at night, but more importantly, it was dry – good for the giant bonfire that had been erected in the main castle courtyard.

This was a good way to get rid of all the junk of the castle that had accumulated over the year. The adults didn't even have to collect it from the nooks and crannies (concealed areas) as the young boys Rory, wee Charlie and Pally Ally included, all had a sixth sense for finding anything that was flammable and putting it on the bonfire. The adult's problem was recovering any valuable item from the bonfire before it was lit, and keeping an eye on the wagon they were repairing, or on the prize broom that they had left unattended.

The Constable needed his eagle eyes to keep an eye on all of them, because if it wasn't nailed down it was gone, and even then, it might be gone if it was loose. The main problem for Rory, Charlie and Ally was finding a costume for the "guising". Charlie, being small had acquired a sheep's sheared fleece from his Dad's estate but he was a bit concerned that he might be the butt of a few jokes dressed in it.

Ally, being skinny, with his shock of red hair, thought that he would be a bright spark and go as a matchstick. Rory had enlisted the aid of his Mum and an old white sheet and some left-over wool from Charlie to make a beard, to dress up as a Druid.

All had great fun scooping out a tumshie (turnip), to make a scary lantern with a small candle in it to light it up. The Monks were organising a party for all the school children for All Hallows' Day, in the refectory, with games of apple "dooking" or "dunking" (retrieving an apple from a bucket of water using only one's mouth) or attempting to eat, while blindfolded, a treacle coated scone hanging on a piece of string. One game got you very wet whilst the other got you very sticky. The clever children went for the treacle first, and got cleaned in the water afterwards.

Night came and all the apprentices Rory, Pally Ally and Angus, all got dressed in their costumes and they met at the foundry, before heading out to see the bonfire being lit.

Rory was taken aback when he saw Angus, who was now classed as an adult, since his initiation going to the fancy dress ball in the Great Hall. He was dressed in fine red silk pyjamas printed with a pattern of a dragon, and a red circular hat with the same design.

Both had been practising the unarmed fighting techniques everyday together. Angus had told Rory that many from his Clan (MacDonald) learned it and that no other Clan knew the techniques. It had been passed down from the Warrior Maiden Scáthach the Shadow who had stayed at his home in Dunscaith Castle and who was the daughter of the mysterious Bruce[6]. Angus only taught Rory as they were friends and he needed someone to practice with.

---

6 Scáthach the Shadow, legendary Scottish warrior woman and martial arts teacher, trained the Irish Celtic Hero Cú Chulainn in the arts of combat. Excerpt from Wikipedia.

Angus noticed that Rory and Ally were curious about his unusual clothing, and he told them that they came from Scáthach's Clan, who came from far away and that he had found them when he was young, in a chest at Dunscaith Castle. Rory asked Angus what he was "guising" at in that outfit, and he laughed and said, "A China Man". Rory and Ally gave one another a quizzical look, thinking of a man made of china and these puzzled looks made Angus laugh even more.

Rory and Ally lit their scary lanterns painted with pictures of ghosts and ghouls, and they both walked away to see the bonfire being lit. Angus left them to meet a lassie he said that he was going to jump through the smoke with[7].

Angus was behaving very strangely Rory thought, as he saw him meet with a tall pretty lassie with jet black hair. She had strange dark eyes, and she moved very gracefully, dressed in a ball gown, and she looked like a princess would from a modern day Disney movie. Rory hadn't seen her before in the castle, but he had seen a ship of visitors arrive for the ball, and he assumed she must have been with them.

Just then, a sheep came running up to Rory and it began butting at his legs. Druid Rory looked down from below his hood and itchy beard at Wee Charlie, who did make a very convincing sheep.

As he was laughing at the sheep, a young witch flew towards him. It was Heather, broom and all. She com-

---

7 Tradition to ward off evil spirits.

mented on being a white witch, not a black evil one who was the enemy of the Druids, and she tried to give Rory a kiss. Fortunately for Rory her, long false warty nose got in the way long enough for him to dodge out the way.

Ally said that he wanted to see if they needed a light for the bonfire as all the school mates of ghosts and ghouls who had congregated to compare costumes burst out laughing. Ally's hint must have worked, as the bonfire went up with a "whoosh," lighting up the interior of the castle in an orange/red light.

The hoard of monsters and witches headed for the service door to the main kitchen. Everyone knew that that was where the best purvey (food) was to be had, and they were not disappointed as Mrs Paterson opened the door holding a large tray covered in toffee apples. Everyone was soon munching them after telling jokes or singing a song for Mrs Paterson and her staff. Pockets and cloth bags were soon filled with nuts and savoury and sweet treats, as they split into groups trying to outdo one another, to the next destination for the best treat. Every occupied dwelling place had something special for them.

A special batch of sweet ginger wine awaited them at the brewery behind the foundry, with candy from Murdo Hands at the stables. Even the Constable had the door to the gatehouse open with more nuts and sweets. Everyone's bags were bursting as they walked to the refectory for more goodies and a party, after blackening their faces with cooled ash from the edges of the bonfire for good luck.

As Rory passed the bonfire he saw Angus and the mystery young woman jump through a plume of smoke, blowing towards them in the night breeze. Angus saw Rory approaching and he began talking to the woman who he called Esther, which was the only word Rory could understand, as they spoke in a very strange language.

She turned towards him and gave him a beautiful smile that lit up her heart shaped face. Rory was captivated by her smile, and Esther noticed this as she spoke to Angus in their secret language, causing him to laugh again as they had obviously talked about him.

Rory watched as the couple stood together and threw two large chestnuts into the edge of the fire, which popped and jumped together. Rory understood this from today's school lessons on All Hallows, on the practice of divination, which was very popular. Had the nuts jumped apart, Rory would not have seen them move close together and hold hands, as they would not be destined to be together. As the nuts moved together he knew to give them some privacy, and walked off looking for a match and a sheep.

This was a happy time for all the children as they dunked for apples and got covered in treacle from the hanging scones in the refectory. Rory was stuffed with sweets and treacle scones, as Heather walked up to him from a large group of girls who had been whispering and giggling together. She was holding an apple and a knife, and she carved a length of skin off the apple, and she then turned her back to him and threw it over her left shoulder. It landed at Rory's feet and it curled into the shape of the letter R[8]. Heather turned, and she stared at the peel and then she ran away giggling.

'Now what was that all about,' thought Rory?

---

8 A traditional Scottish form of divining one's future spouse is to carve an apple in one long strip, then toss the peel over one's shoulder. The peel is believed to land in the shape of the first letter of the future spouse's name.

CHAPTER 5

Time

Winter came with a vengeance to the Highlands and Urquhart Castle. Fortunately, with the good summer and the plentiful harvest, the huge storage rooms in the basements below the castle buildings were full to overflowing. The basements were always cold, being below ground level and surrounded by the heavy damp stone walls. Even in the middle of summer, it was cold and a perfect place for keeping all produce and meat, as long as the rooms were secure and free of rats. The store master of the castle had contacted the local farms and crofters and had purchased several cats from them, to control the increase in rats infecting the storerooms. The trouble now was that there were too many cats!

The kitchen was very busy, preserving all manner of foodstuffs, as well as making jam from the harvest of brambleberries. These had been collected from the area surrounding the castle and Castletoun, by the children and the women. There was no shortage of food as the livestock was brought down from the high fields and housed in byres at the local farms, where a bumper crop of feed was stored. Fishing never stopped and was easily landed at the water gate to the castle, and it supplemented the diet of the population.

The first blizzard of the year hit at the start of December, covering the ground with snow which was soon rolled into giant snowmen by the children, with the paths being cleared by the army of adults all working together. The stockpiles of food and fuel from the log and peat stacked mountains, would easily last for the winter months and well into the spring, when the cycle of growing began again. The organisation of the castle was very good, and it had to be, for the population to survive the harsh conditions of a Scottish winter.

Carpenters were busy producing carved wooden toys, including spinning tops and sap whistles, for Christmas gifts for the children, giving them additional income with even Hamish and the blacksmiths being assisted by the apprentices of Angus, Ally and Rory making metal hoops for rolling with a stick.[9]

This was a good skill to learn as the principles were the same for making cart wheels, only on a smaller scale.

Christmas came with great excitement and the expectation of gifts with even the poorest child receiving something. A special food treat for Christmas dinner was a stuffed Canadian goose from the large unexpected flock who had flown in to winter in Scotland, or the large Turkeys bred at a local farm. The rich Clootie Dumpling and puddings made sure that no one would waste away, by providing that extra insulation around the waist.

Rory was busy putting his new skills to work under the instruction of Hamish, and he made his first metal fire companion set for his Mum. It comprised a bucket,

---

9 Known as a Gird and cleek or Girdle.

poker, hand shovel and toasting fork on a stand, and he polished them to a high shine. Hamish was very pleased with the standard of Rory's work and he was progressively giving him more and more difficult tasks.

On Christmas morning, Rory woke to a pile of presents outside his door, with new clothes from his Mum, which he badly needed, a spinning top, a wooden whistle and a new set of knuckle bones (a game played with five sheep knuckle bones thrown in the air and caught on the back of the hand) from Hamish and the other blacksmiths, Jimmy and Gordon.

Rory was very happy and was going to have Christmas dinner with his Mum and brother Johnny in Grant Tower, while his stepdad was entertaining Clan Chiefs at a feast in the Great Hall. He re-wrapped the whistle as a gift for Johnny, which he knew he would like, and he put it with his Mum's present.

Everyone got dressed in their best clothes and went to a special Christmas Day service in the temple, conducted by the Abbot. All the children were there and took a present down to the front of the altar, where the Abbot took it in turns, playing with their toys, whilst preaching about the reason for exchanging gifts on this day. It was a very joyous service, and everyone was very happy and smiling.

Rory saw his mum with his stepdad who looked happy for a change and a smiling Johnny holding a new Gird and Cleek, which Rory recognised as the one that he had made. At the end of the service, everyone left wishing one another and the Abbot a Merry Christmas at the door.

As Rory approached the Abbot, he saw him take a wrapped book out from inside his Robe, and he gave it to Rory. Everyone was looking. The Abbot was giving Rory a present and wishing him a Merry Christmas; he must be very special, they all thought; no one gets a present from the Abbot. They usually give him presents!

Rory unwrapped it to find a new Bible with a pressed image of Saint Columba on the black leather front cover.

The Abbot said, "This will aid your studies Rory;" And he gave him a wink. Rory quickly hid it in his plaid until he was alone to look at it.

Every night he read his new Bible which was very special indeed, as it was also a condensed version of the book of Saint Columba that the Abbot had. The monks had painstakingly copied it. Excerpts of Rory's future were contained in it, and he saw himself looking out from pages from some very strange locations.

Time passed quickly for Rory as he devoted his life to learning all his new skills, and he soaked up as much education as possible, just like a sponge soaking up water. He was growing fast, and could hardly wait for the events in the book he had seen to unfold and happen.

Spring came, followed by summer, autumn and winter and back to spring, and to summer again, as Rory had six birthdays. He was now fourteen years old, and he was a muscular six-foot young man. The special haggis from Granny Grant had done its job, and he was very strong, and could work the metal as well as all the other blacksmiths. Granny looked like she hadn't aged a day, and Rory still couldn't figure out how old she was.

Angus was now twenty-two, and an expert at making guns and he was showing Rory how to do it. They had become great friends and he had invited Rory to come to Dunscaith Castle for his wedding to Esther, the girl who he had jumped the smoke with six years before, at Halloween.

He had asked Rory to be his best man, which was a great honour and one he was looking forward to. Pally Ally (Allister MacAllister), the other apprentice was now nineteen, and he had filled out to a muscular six-foot-tall, handsome man, since he had lost all his plooks (spots). Ally had had his manhood initiation three years before, and he was now full of confidence at fighting off all the young women of the castle and Castletoun, and he was out with a different one every night.

This gave the other Blacksmiths Jimmy Black and Gordon Grant much hilarity, recalling their youth and womanising days, as they cracked jokes with Ally, and gave him advice about women. This advice when he used it, usually got him a slap from the latest young woman who he was dating, to their great amusement!

Wee Charlie Campbell was still small for his fourteen years, being only five feet six, but he had become an expert horseman after his initial set back. He became an apprentice of Murdo Hands the head stableman. He had learned the trade of the Saddler, working leather and making reins, saddles and all leather goods, and he had a knack (gift) for it. He wanted to be in Rory's company at every opportunity and he considered himself his special friend, although he was always seen in the company of groups of castle girls, laughing and joking with them.

Hamish Cooper, the head Smithy, was now very happy and a lot heavier since marrying his whisky tasting partner the widow Moira Paterson, two years before, and moving into her spacious quarters above the main kitchen in the castle. It was a lavish wedding conducted by the Abbot in the Chapel, with Heather now a pretty fourteen-year-old, all dolled up in a posh frock and she made a very beautiful bridesmaid.

It was the party of a lifetime in the Great Hall, with all the castle residents and friends of the happy couple from further afield, in attendance. The Great Hall had been specially prepared with the Lord and Lady Grant and visiting dignitaries at the top table on the left of the hall, along with the bride and groom and the Abbot and the bridesmaid Heather.

Both sides of the huge hall with its wooden beamed ceiling and walls, were bedecked with tapestries. Below them were cloth covered benches and seats for all the visiting guests. A large dance floor was in the middle, with the live band on the high wooden stage on the right. Heather's eye was still firmly on Rory, who she visited daily at the foundry with a big basket of food, to keep his strength up. She made sure that Rory danced with her and he seemed to enjoy it after about the tenth dance. Heather was very happy to have a new Dad who spoiled her rotten, and she was glad to see her Mum so happy.

If only Rory's Mum was as happy, but unfortunately, she looked haggard now, with dark patches below her eyes. Johnny was now ten and he was behaving like a right brat. He was still spoiled by his Dad John Grant, and given special treatment at school, with a blind eye being turned to his bullying of the other kids of his own age, and even younger.

Rory's Stepdad John Grant didn't dare beat his wife any longer after Rory had stood up to him when visiting his Mum; when he saw his stepdad raise his hand to her. At six feet now with a muscular physique, he towered over John Grant, who had backed down, and had stormed off to the Great Hall to drink more whisky. That was a few weeks ago now, and he still got drunk, but he had never dared to hit his Mum since.

Rory thought that he would have a quiet word with Johnny about his conduct, as he appeared to be the only person in the castle who was not afraid of his stepdad. Johnny needed to be put straight about his behaviour, and he knew that Rory would enforce his words if they went unheeded. His father John Grant had no influence over Rory, and Johnny was aware of the consequences if he ran "greetin" (crying) to him, as he would have to face more than a few more words from Rory!

Fitba (football) was very popular now, with teams from outlying villages and towns coming to play in a competition on Saturdays. The field had been properly converted into a sports area, with wooden goal posts erected at each end, with taller goal posts extending from it into the air for the new game Rory, Angus, Ally and Charlie had invented.

The ball had burst one day, and it was filled with straw, which made it into an oblong shape. The field was really muddy, and Rory ran, carrying the ball towards the posts. Wee Charlie raced after him and he dived forward, catching Rory by his legs, but not before he threw the ball backwards behind him to Ally, who was running up behind him. The ball spun round in the air and it was caught by Ally, who carried on running towards the posts.

Angus was in front of Ally, and he was determined that he was not going to let him pass, but a piece of nifty footwork left Angus nose deep in mud, and the ball below the post. Ally took the ball back to where Angus was face down in the mud and threw it at him, laughing. Angus got up and in a fit of anger at being bested kicked the ball at the posts. It flew over the top of them to much cheering and jesting from all who were watching.

Unknown to them, the new game would later be known as Rugby!

There was a serious side to the daily routine, as Rory became highly developed in his skills and he was now learning the advanced techniques of the foundry, making gun barrels. First, he placed the iron ore in the furnace where it was melted and cleaned of all impurities by puddling.[10] He then used a pair of tongs to grab a ball of ore and manipulated it with a tilt hammer until it was a square shaped block. His arm muscles were bulging as

10 This is when the impurities in the ore which are generally lighter than the molten iron rise to the top and can be skimmed off. The iron is then cooled and formed into large balls called blooms.

he hammered the block[11] and made the additional impurities and brittle scale fly off. He then rolled the metal, thinning it and increasing the ductility of the iron bar, making it suitable for making gun barrels.

Rory enjoyed the peace and the calm that came over him when he worked the metal and he enjoyed the challenge and he could daydream as he worked. He was looking forward to the boat trip to Dunscaith Castle on Skye, as he had never left Urquhart Castle before.

Angus helped Rory to cut the steel and the iron bars into equal lengths, and then arranged them into layers and they worked together, taking turns to weld them together by hitting them with their heavy hammers. Both talked of the forthcoming wedding and Angus said that he was more nervous of that than of his initiation all those years ago when they had first become friends. They continued to work, heating and welding more bars together until they were at a red-hot heat, with Angus putting one end into a fixed square hole on the work bench, as Rory pulled the other end with tongs and twisted, making sure that it twisted evenly, until they had the starting point of a gun barrel.

Angus had asked Rory if he would stay at Dunscaith Castle for a while, to help him set up a new foundry. Although still young, Rory had the mental attitude of someone much older, and he was excited about this. He had learnt as much as he could there, but he would have to ask the Abbot first.

---

11 The Process is called Shingling.

Rory had become very close to the Abbot, who was like a second father to him. They had spent a lot of time together, studying the Book of Saint Columba. It contained a full account of Rory's future, as seen through the premonitions of Saint Columba and it had more information than Rory's condensed version. One of the obscure chapters that he had been shown, was now starting to make sense.

It was a picture of an adult-sized Rory remaking a sword in a heavy stone foundry. The picture of him on the next page was very strange indeed; of him digging in an alien landscape of rock and dirt. One thing that was familiar to the Abbot was that the Rory in the pictures was the same Rory as the young man standing in front of him now.

Rory explained the offer from Angus, to the Abbot, to accompany him to Dunscaith Castle on Skye to set up a new foundry. The Abbot flicked through the book of Saint Columba back to the picture of Rory at the same age, where he was remaking the sword in a strange large stone room, with a large foundry, with massive bellows and he showed it to Rory.

"You are destined to go and remake the sword there," said the Abbot.

Rory said that he had seen that picture in his condensed version, and he agreed with the Abbot.

"You don't need to worry about money. You are already wealthy from the haggis tusks you gave me six years ago," said the Abbot.

He gave Rory a small bag of mixed gold and copper coins and a credit note for £50, which was comparative to about £5000, by today's standards.

"This should be enough for your needs, and you can cash the credit note at the nearest monastery if you need to, but you must return to Urquhart Castle before your sixteenth birthday, as not all of the pictures in the book of Saint Columba are in your special Bible. You can't know everything that is going to happen," exclaimed the Abbot with a smile.

CHAPTER 6

The Trip

It was a fine warm sunny Scottish summer's day in July when Roddy MacLeod the Captain of the MacLeod Clan Ship (Birlinn Class) named The Stag from Stornoway, sailed down Loch Ness to Urquhart Castle. It was so named for the prize Stag's head mounted at the front of the ship, which he had hunted, and was very proud of. It carried on towards the huge castle standing proudly on the protruding rocky outcrop of land, jutting out on the water, against the view of the right bank of the Loch, lit by the sun overhead.

Captain Roddy barked orders to the crew who lowered the sails and rowed the ship to the quay, anchoring it at the water gate entrance to the castle. The Stag was a small twelve oar vessel built for speed, and for the conveyance of light goods, and it was one of the fastest in the fleet of ships owned by the Lord of the Isles of Lewis and Harris, Torquil MacLeod.[12]

---

12 The birlinn spelt birlinn in Scottish Gaelic) was a wooden vessel propelled by sail and oar, used extensively in the Hebrides and West Highlands of Scotland from the Middle Ages on. Variants of the name in English and Lowland Scots include "berlin" and "birling". The Gallo-Norse term may have been derived from the Norse byrðingr (ship of burden). It has been suggested that a local design lineage might also be traceable to vessels similar to the Broighter-type boat (first century BC), equipped with

The Lord of Isle of Lewis and Harris had a considerable fleet of ships, including the larger West Highland galleys. For over four hundred years, down to the seventeenth century, the Birlinn was the dominant vessel in the Hebrides. The distinction was between galleys, having between eighteen and twenty oars, and birlinn's, with between twelve and eighteen oars. There were no structural differences, with three men per oar.

oars and a square sail, without the need to assume a specific Viking design influence. The majority of scholars emphasize the Viking influence on the birlinn which was clinker-built (where the edges of hull planks overlap), called a "land" or "landing," and it could be sailed or rowed. It had a single mast holding the square sail. Smaller vessels of this type might have had as few as twelve oars.

All the lords of the Isles[13] had their own fleets of galleys and smaller birlinns, and the current lord of the Islands of Lewis and Harris, Torquil MacLeod was no exception. He was a descendant from a series of hybrid Viking/Gaelic rulers of the West Coast and Islands of Scotland, who welded their sea power with fleets of Galleys. This allowed them to remain functionally independent for many centuries. Torquil MacLeod and the other lords from the Islands of the Hebrides and Skye and the west coast mainland of Ross, Knoydart, Ardnamurchan and the Kintyre peninsula were the greatest landowners, and the most powerful lords in the British Isles, after the Kings of Scotland and England.

Captain Roddy MacLeod was in his late forties and only five feet six; the same height as Charlie, due to his bandy legs, which he said gave him great stability aboard ship. He was still an impressive figure with his short greying dark hair, covered with a dark cap and dressed in a short sleeved white shirt, showing his highly muscled forearms[14], he was the father of Esther, his only child to his wife of twenty five years Lee Chan MacLeod, who was a direct descendant of Scáthach the Shadow, the legendary Scottish warrior woman who had married Angus Og MacDonald, the cousin of the Lord of Skye, generations before. He was very protective and proud of his

---

13 Scottish Gaelic: Triath nan Eilean or Rìgh Innse Gall is a title of Scottish nobility with historical roots that go back beyond the Kingdom of Scotland.

14 Put a pipe in his mouth and a tin of spinach in his hand and he could pass for Popeye.

daughter, and he wanted to check out his future son-in-law Angus, to see if he was suitable to marry her. If he was not, he would be having something to say about it.

Angus too, was very nervous about the meeting and he wanted to make a good impression. Captain Roddy was the brother of the Lord of the Isles of Lewis and Harris, Torquil MacLeod, and making a good impression was a very good idea. The truce between the Clans of MacLeod and MacDonald hung in the balance, with this marriage.

It would be further cemented with the marriage of Angus to Esther, as he was the Son of the Lord of the Isle of Skye, Eoin (Iain) MacDonald, whose sister Martha was married to the brother of Roddy's wife Lee Chan. The wedding was causing a lot of excitement for Captain Roddy's wife Lee Chan MacLeod, who was looking forward to the family reunion with her only brother Bruce, named after the father of Scáthach. He still resided at Dunscaith Castle with his wife Martha (the sister of Lord Eoin MacDonald), and his children young Bruce and Jacqueline Lee Chan, known as Jacqui (Jackie). This would be the first family reunion of all the surviving direct descendants of Scáthach the Shadow, the legendary Scottish Warrior Woman.

It had been years since Lee Chan's brother Bruce had visited and stayed at Stornoway Castle, along with his children and his wife Martha and young Angus, on holiday. He had gone to give advice and to train the blacksmiths there, on making cannons and gunpowder, as part of the union between the Clans. This was when Angus had first met his second cousin Esther, who he immediately got on with and they were as thick as thieves as children. Lee Chan was looking forward to seeing her brother's children, young Bruce and Jackie again, who had by now grown into teenagers.

The skills of sword making and alchemy had been brought from China by Scáthach's father. He had been given the western name of Bruce by his mysterious rescuer, and it had been passed down to the first male child. Along with the knowledge of how to make gunpowder this had made the MacDonald Clan very powerful.

These was the main reasons why the Macleod's and MacDonald's had formed their first marriage truce with the family of Lee Chan, who possessed this knowledge, and who had prevented a bloody war between the two Clans.

Angus was at the pier, accompanied by Rory, to provide moral support as his future father-in-law Captain Roddy disembarked from the Stag. He walked up to him with his bandy leg gait, as if he were still being rocked side to side by the waves. He came straight up to Angus, eyeing him up and down, and reached out his right hand.

This quickly changed into a two-handed shake of the hands, which looked a bit strange to Rory, but Captain Roddy's face lit up with recognition. They both whispered something to one another, finishing with Captain Roddy giving Angus a strong cuddle, and calling him son. Rory was intrigued at the change of atmosphere between them, which had gone from tense and icy to warm and friendly, within seconds. Something had happened between them, but it was lost on Rory. The Captain shouted at his crew on the ship, granting them shore leave until eight a.m. the next day.

Rory was almost trampled in the rush, as they ran down the gangplank and along the pier towards the water gate, and into the castle, looking for an inn or a bar for a drink. They were quickly stopped in their tracks as the huge frame of the Constable appeared out of the shadows at the entrance. Weapons were surrendered as they were politely informed of the ground rules of behaviour, by the Constable. They were also, not so politely, informed of the consequences of their failure to comply. The sailors then rapidly dispersed, to continue to Castletoun in their search for a drink and a bit of womanly companionship!

Angus introduced Rory to Captain Roddy, who gave him a normal one-handed shake of the hand. Both Angus and his future father-in-law seemed best pals already, as they all walked to the foundry, where the Captain was introduced to all the blacksmiths Hamish, Gordon, Jimmy and Ally, who all exchanged the funny two-handed shake with the Captain and whispered together. Rory was definitely the odd one out, as they laughed and joked together!

Hamish told the Captain that he could sleep in his old room above the foundry that night as 'The Stag' wasn't leaving until tomorrow's current and tide. He then invited him back to the brewery to sample some of the new beers that they had been brewing, and to do some whisky tasting, followed by a visit to the refectory for some more hospitality. They had just tapped a new brew which had a good kick at 8.9% ABV (Alcohol by Volume) and named it the Stag, after Captain Roddy's ship. He was very pleased, and he gratefully accepted a pint of it, followed by another. It was some time later that they all Stag-erred (staggered), off together, laughing and joking, to the refectory with Hamish telling Rory to tidy up at the forge.

Rory finished off all the half-completed jobs that had been left and banked the fire to keep it lit overnight. He packed his bag with his clothes, his apron, his gauntlets and the specialised tools that he would need. He carefully wrapped the broken sword in the heavy red cloth that he recovered it in, making sure that no pieces were missing, and he tied it securely with the red cord dangling from it. He then went to his bed for the night, to be fresh for his trip the next day. It was late when he was awakened by all the drunks noisily returning, still laughing and banging about, trying to get to their beds.

As Rory was up first at dawn, he attended to the fire and he started making a big pot of porridge for the hungover apparitions slowly staggering down the stairs from the quarters above the foundry. A cold wash and belly of porridge restored all the blacksmiths and the Captain, who seemed remarkably sober, compared with the others, trying to return to a semblance of normality. He said that it was his sea legs that enabled him to hold his drink. Rory had seen Hamish, Gordon and Jimmy take a good bucketful of drink before, but they looked really rough, compared to the Captain. Angus was positively green about the gills, but he was putting on a brave face to impress the Captain, and to show him that he was not a wimp (weakling).

It was then time to go and catch the outward current to the river Ness, which would save the ship from being rowed. The weather was so good that Rory and Angus dressed in one of their one-piece short sleeved white shirts, and their half clan kilts, and sporrans, holding their valuables, with light woollen knee-length socks and holding their Sgian Dubh with leather strap sandals on their feet.[15]

Rory and Angus collected their belongings and, accompanied by Hamish, Gordon, Jimmy and Ally, they all walked to the pier, to board the Stag with the Captain.

As they passed though the water gate, Rory was amazed to see it lined on either side with all his friends, including wee Charlie and all the castle residents and staff. He saw Murdo Hands from the stables next to Charlie, who was crying like a wee lassie and being consoled by Pooie Doo (Father Doogan). They were standing with the Abbot and the huge figure of the Constable John Gregg, who was next to the small hunched figure of Granny Grant.

Rory's eyes filled with tears at this send-off and he was not the only one that was "greetin" (crying) as Heather came running up to him, jumping into his arms and gave him a big kiss on the lips. A new emotion hit Rory who was growing up fast, as he felt a strange stirring in him as

---

15 The Sgian Dubh is a small, single-edged knife (Gaelic Sgian), worn as part of the traditional Scottish Highland dress, along with the kilt. Originally used for eating and preparing fruit, meat, and cutting bread and cheese, as well as serving for other more general day to day uses such as cutting material and protection, it is now worn as part of traditional Scottish dress tucked into the top of the kilt hose (sock) with only the Upper portion of the hilt visible. The Sgian Dubh is normally worn on the same side as the dominant hand.

he kissed her back. She made him promise to come back safe and sound to her, and she had to be practically prised out of his arms by Hamish her protective new stepdad. She moved into her Mum's arms the now Mrs Cooper, no longer the widow Paterson, where she wept uncontrollably on her shoulder, at Rory's leaving.

Rory's mum Mary was waiting at the gangplank with his wee brother Johnny, who came up to Rory and gave him a warm cuddle. The "talk" that Rory had given him had worked, he thought, and Johnny was far better behaved now. Rory made him promise to look after his Mum, which he sincerely said he would do, which helped to relieve some of Rory's anxiety.

The last person to embrace Rory was his Mum, Mary who was very small now in comparison to him, as they both cuddled and cried, and she also made him promise to be careful and to look after himself.

Rory eventually joined the Captain and Angus on the foredeck of The Stag, which cast off from the wharf. It moved into the strong current, travelling towards the north of the Loch and the exit to the wide deep river Ness. Everyone stayed on the pier, waving, and in the case of Heather and his Mum, crying, as they travelled up the Loch and out of view.

It was great weather for Rory's first trip on a ship as it was carried along on the current, without the need of any aid, giving the hung-over crew a chance to recover from all the cheap beer and whisky that they had consumed in the taverns of Castletoun. The ship approached Lochend, went into Loch Dochfour and steered into the deep left channel of the river Ness, passing the twin islands situated in the centre of the river. The ship carried on through the city of Inverness along the wide river, over-looked by the castle, occupied by the Scottish Army on the hill on their right.

This was the first time that Rory had seen a major city!

The capital of the Highlands was a mass of people and carts as the business of the day was carried out at both street stalls, and in impressive stone buildings on the right side of the river. The river was busy now with other large and smaller boats crossing it, as Captain Roddy barked orders to his crew, which were instantly obeyed. The Stag exited into the Beauly Firth Harbour mouth, past all the berthed ships loading and unloading their goods. This was a rich city and it was obvious why with all these expen-sive items were being traded.

Once out in the open sea Captain Roddy ordered the sails to be raised which powered The Stag forwards up the East Coast of Scotland towards the Island of Kirkwall and left between the small Islands of Stroma and Swona. The Island of Hoy was on the right, where the rocky old man of Hoy stood like a large finger pointing towards the sky.

The most northerly part of the Scottish mainland and Dunnet Head was passed on the left, as Rory ran from left to right, looking at the mass of wildlife in the sea of Minke, Humpback, fin, killer, pilot and sperm whales and pods of Dolphins and porpoises, swimming alongside the ship; who all appeared to be as interested in Rory as he was in them. The secluded bays had otters and grey seals basking in the sun, with puffins and all sorts of sea birds flying past. Rory had never seen these creatures before, and Captain Roddy was amused at his antics, behaving like a small inquisitive child, but he patiently explained what each creature was, and he was secretly pleased at the interest that Rory was showing. The creatures of the sea seemed to be as interested in Rory as he was in them, and swam alongside the Stag.

A shout of alarm went up from the lookout at the front of the ship, as a massive shadow covered it. If a blanket had been placed over you on a bright sunny day then it would describe the experience! This was the first time that Rory had seen any fear shown by the crew and he looked up.

The largest bird he had ever seen was hovering above the ship, as the crew rushed to get long spears. Rory recognised this bird, it was now fully grown and bigger than the ship and its highly intelligent eyes were looking straight at him, as if waiting for a signal. It was Ben the Great Scottish Eagle, who had taken him for the ride of his life when he had the Hagpipe[16].

Rory no longer had the Hagpipe and he didn't know if he could communicate with the eagle without it, but he had to try for the safety of the ship and the crew. Rory stared straight at Ben and into its eyes and gave a slight bow, the same as Ben had when they had first met. Ben immediately recognised Rory, and he let out a loud

---

16 Read Book 1: Rory Mac Sween and the Secrets of Urquhart Castle.

squawk, which vibrated in the air around the ship, sending everyone into a complete panic as the crew dived below the rowing boards for protection from the huge talons silently hovering in the air above their heads. They knew that if the bird attacked they would stand no chance, and even the wooden boards would provide little protection and would be ripped apart like balsa wood (soft paper like wood).

No one was watching as the crew cowered in fear as Rory stood firm, looking at Ben who returned a slight nod of his head, in reply to Rory's bow. He gave a silent flap of his powerful wings and flew off, circling the ship. Captain Roddy was the only one who had not run for cover, and he had watched this encounter. He came up to Rory and gave him a slap on the back.

"That was either the bravest or the most stupid thing I have ever seen. Do you know what that was?" he asked.

Rory replied, "A Great Scottish Eagle I saw one once before when I was little."

The Captain scratched his head, and he explained that it had been terrorising the shipping there for the last six years, as if looking for something, and then he said, "And I think today it has found it!"

The rest of the journey was uneventful, except for the left turn into the Minch, where the North Sea collides with the hot waters from the North Atlantic Drift.[17] To say it is choppy where these currents meet is an under-

---

17 Well hotter than the North Sea!

statement, and Rory discovered at this time that he did not have sea legs yet, and definitely not a sea stomach.

He was very pleased to see Stornoway Harbour on the Island of Lewis approaching, and he was desperate to get his feet onto dry land!

CHAPTER 7

Stornoway

Rory was as green as the grass on the hills when The Stag sailed into the fortified stone harbour of Stornoway.[18]

They passed a very busy shipyard full of workers, where a very squeamish Rory saw that many new vessels were under construction. Work stopped as the ship workers waved to their friends, and relatives on board the ships. Rory fought the retching afflicting, him not wanting to throw up in front of this audience. Fortunately, he was not noticed in the excitement of the return of Captain Roddy and his crew!

The main harbour was full of Galleys and Birlinns and fishing boats, berthed at the quays of Stornoway Town which was a hive of activity with people going about their daily business. The town had a central square which was the communal meeting point for the residents and visitors. Its narrow streets all converged on this square if you walked in the general direction of the harbour, and it was impossible to get lost there. Many taverns and pubs were situated in and around the square, and were doing a roaring trade from all the sailors and traders visiting.

---

18 Historic Note, it was founded in the ninth century by the Vikings. Norse name Stjornavagr.

The Stag's sail was lowered as the crew rowed it into the inner harbour, into the waters of Bayhead where the looming ancient castle of the MacLeod Clan was situated on its left. She was berthed at her own well-guarded private quay in very quick time. Rory had to be helped across the gangplank by Angus, in case he fell into the sea, as his legs were still very wobbly. Even when on solid ground he could still feel the ground swaying below him and he was causing some amusement to the Captain and the crew, as he heard them laugh and mutter "landlubber."

Rory looked up from the spinning ground to see a bemused welcoming committee, including Esther MacLeod, Angus's fiancée.

She was wearing a figure-hugging red and blue dress on her striking, slim five-foot ten-inch frame, with her beautiful slightly oriental heart-shaped face, framed with shiny black shoulder-length hair. She was accompanied by a shorter more rotund woman, about five-foot six inches tall, the same as her husband Captain Roddy. Lee Chan McLeod had slightly stronger oriental features, with slightly greying shoulder-length black hair, which was tied behind her head, and she was wearing a full-length dark dress. It was hard for Rory to tell her age, but she looked too young to be to be Esther's mother.

Roddy's face lit up on seeing his wife and daughter, who ran to him, exchanging kisses and cuddles. Esther then turned to Angus and started speaking to him in a language that Rory couldn't understand. He had studied hard and could speak fluently in Gaelic, Latin, Norse, French and English but he couldn't understand one word of what she was saying to Angus, but he guessed that it must be personal, by the blush on his face. Angus then surprised Rory by replying in the same language (Mandarin), to Esther.

Rory decided that he was going to pay attention and learn this strange language, feeling that it was important, and that it would also be a lot of fun to be in on this secret. Angus turned to Rory and introduced him to his fiancée, whose face lit up with a beautiful smile, causing Rory to stutter a "hello," much to her amusement. Captain Roddy told both Angus and Rory that they were staying with him in his quarters in the castle and he instructed two of his crew to bring their belongings.

Rory was still unsteady on his feet and feeling sick, as he followed the Captain, his wife, Angus and Esther; both arm in arm into the ancient castle, over a drawbridge and a moat, to very spacious rooms, and a kitchen in the main keep, near to its great hall. A very strange smell was in the air, like nothing Rory had ever smelt before, and he was feeling quite ill when he sat down in the kitchen.

This was not lost on Lee Chan, who must have noticed his green colour, as she gave him a small china cup containing a hot fluid, and said, "Drink, Drink."

Rory took a sip and he felt the liquid burn all the way down his gullet, but almost immediately, he felt a lot better, and he took another sip of the rice flavoured drink. This was the first time that he had tried Sake, and he quite liked it.[19]

He watched Lee Chan with great interest, as Esther helped her prepare a meal which he did not recognise. Both Angus and Roddy had a china cup in their hand and a glazed clay bottle in front of them, which was sitting in a bowl of hot water. It dawned on Captain Roddy that this was all a new experience to Rory and he explained that he was going to be eating Chinese food. He said it was almost as popular in Stornoway as the MacLeod black pudding.

His wife Lee Chan had opened a shop in the town, where a lot of people came to buy carry-out, to take to their homes to eat with their families. Rory had to admit that he really enjoyed it but wanted more a short time later. The first "Carry Out" Chinese food had begun!

Both Rory and Angus bunked together in a spacious room with two single feather mattress beds, next to the room shared by Captain Roddy and his wife; with Esther's room on the other side of that. The corridor in between had very squeaky floor boards, which let out a very loud noise when stood on. The Captain liked Angus, but there would be no hanky panky (not

---

19 The making of Rice Wine a Chinese alcoholic beverage pre-dates recorded history. In the Yellow River area, bronze vessels for heating and serving alcoholic beverages survive from the later Shang dynasty whose oracle bones contained the first surviving Chinese characters including the word for alcoholic beverages.

a Chinese word but a Scottish one for misbehaviour) under his roof!

Rory awoke from a wonderful night's sleep on the feather mattress which he melted into. He would have to get one of these. It was far better than rolling about on a lumpy horsehair one. Angus was already awake, and had returned to the room, as Rory was getting washed, using a jug of water at the sink in the corner of the room. It was connected to the outside wall by a channel and a stopper and soap was left there, along with a fluffy cotton towel.

This was indeed luxury, compared to Urquhart Castle, with the hand pump at the foundry, Rory decided. He saw that Angus was wearing a white heavy cotton jacket and trousers, which were tied with a cord.

He handed Rory the same clothes as he was wearing and a long white hard stiff cotton belt, which he told him to put on for morning practice. Angus explained that they were going to meet Esther in the practice room for Randori (free practice), the weaponless fighting that they had been practicing at Urquhart Castle. Angus showed Rory how to tie the belt twice around his waist, and through a loop in one end, creating a tight flat knot. That way if he fell on it, it would not dig into him. Rory had no intention of falling on it, and he laughed to himself, as he was a lot bigger and stronger than everyone else, except maybe Angus.

Rory put on a pair of sandals and they both walked off along the squeaky corridor to a room at its far end where Esther, Captain Roddy and Lee Chan were waiting, all dressed in the same white suits. Rory noticed that Lee Chan and Esther's belts were black, and that the Captain's belt was brown, and the belt worn by Angus was blue. He asked him what the different colours were for. Angus explained that it was a ranking system which he would explain later! Angus was being a bit devious, as if keeping a secret, and inwardly laughing to himself in good humour, and Rory wondered what was going on.

The room had a large white tarpaulin straw-filled mat covering its entire floor surface, and similar mats around the entire wall surfaces of the room. No part of the room was unpadded and Rory thought, 'why you would need all that padding?' He knew that he was bigger and stronger than Esther and her Mum, but that he might struggle with the Captain but he thought that with his height advantage, he could beat him. He knew from all the practice that he had had with Angus, that they were both evenly matched and he really didn't want to hurt Esther or her Mum.

Rory thought that he had nothing to worry about as he stepped into the room and bowed good morning to Esther and walked towards her. She bowed back and promptly threw him across the room and against the wall, which he was now glad was padded. Rory quickly got up, hearing Angus laughing and walked back onto the mat and towards Lee Chan. She took hold of his suit and threw him across the room to the other wall, back towards Esther.

They began playing ping pong (table tennis) with him, as he flew backwards and forwards across the room between them. Rory knew that he was outmatched, and he could do nothing to prevent himself from being thrown about by Esther and Lee Chan. He slowly got up, catching his breath as Angus told him that when you nod your head it means that you are ready, and never take your eyes off your opponent when you bow.

He said as he laughed, "You had better be careful; appearances can be very deceptive."

Rory was determined not to make the same mistake again as he slowly got to his feet facing Esther for the seventh time, watching her like a hawk. That was absolutely fine as long as he stood still but he decided to try a light strike to her left shoulder with his right palm, trying not to hurt her.

Esther moved like a striking cobra bending and turning below his outstretched arm, taking hold of it throwing him again flat on his back, and this time she followed him to the ground. She took hold of his right arm pulling it over her right leg, as she pinned Rory's head and neck to the ground with her left leg, applying an arm lock and extreme pain to Rory.

Angus shouted, "Tap the mat twice to submit!" which Rory did in quick time.

The hold was released, and Rory again got to his feet, looking at Angus saying, "Are there any other rules that you want to tell me?" as Angus buckled over, laughing at him.

The rest of the practice was conducted by Lee Chan explaining moves and counter moves to Rory at a slow pace. All the years of practice with Angus meant nothing when faced with the expertise of Lee Chan and Esther, and Rory felt like he was back at school again, but he was determined to learn.

It was captain Roddy's turn after morning practice, to show his skills in the kitchen, as he made a full Scottish breakfast for them all, along with fresh bread from the castle bakery. It was a feast of bacon, eggs, slice[20] and fried tattie scones[21] and the world-famous Stornoway black pudding of MacLeod and MacLeod, that was unique to the Island of Lewis.[22]

Rory had never tasted anything like it, and he couldn't decide what food he liked the best between the Chinese and the Scottish!

After breakfast the Captain took Rory and Angus on a guided tour of the castle which was in many ways similar in design and facilities, as Urquhart Castle, except for the roof battlements area overlooking the inner harbour. Surrounding the waters of Bayhead were cannons spaced at regular intervals, covering the whole area. Should any unfriendly sea vessel pass the cannons placed at the fortification at the main harbour they would surely be finished off at the narrow channel to the inner harbour!

Rory paid particular attention to the design and the construction of the cannons, which had an ornate design of a dragon on them. The ancestors of Lee Chan and Esther had been very busy, as the cannons looked very old, but were still in deadly working order.

---

20 Square flat sausage a Scottish delicacy.
21 Another Scottish delicacy made with potatoes and flour.
22 Other MacLeod Black Pudding is Available.

The blacksmiths shop and foundry, although in a very old castle were well maintained and set up specialising in making weapons, with several blacksmiths working at the same time. Rory wondered why they would need so many unless they were constantly at war. This was not far from the truth, as conflicts with other rival Clans and Viking Raiders was commonplace. This strong show of military strength deterred any serious threat, as it would be doomed to failure, making Stornoway one of the most peaceful and prosperous places in the highlands.

Captain Roddy was very proud of his home and rightly so, he took Rory and Angus for a walk in the summer sunshine to Stornoway Town. They went over the retractable bridge at the narrowest part of Bayhead which had guards stationed at all times. No one would catch a MacLeod sleeping on duty, and take them by surprise and again, Rory wondered what had occurred in the past to make them so security conscious.

Stornoway was a very modern town with substantial stone buildings with tiled roofs to cope with the extreme weather of the Highlands and the Islands. It had a sewage system below the pavements, that emptied into the sea, connected to the outside privies (toilet).

The richer houses had their own water supply from their own springs, and did not have the trouble of collecting it from the several wells supplying water to the town which were built on a small hill. It sloped into the flat town centre, with its central square opening onto the main harbour. The Captain took Rory and Angus past the harbour at a very slow pace as he was stopped every couple of minutes by another Captain or crew member, or just a random passer-by wanting to blether (chat or talk) with him. He was a very popular person, Rory realised.

They eventually reached the far end of the harbour which opened onto a smaller second harbour, which was the main shipyard, where two galleys and a birlinn were being constructed. Captain Roddy spent a long time in conversation with the head shipbuilder, talking about the ships using terms like clinks,[23] which was totally lost on Rory. The captain was very happy with the progress being made, with one of the Galley's near completion, and told Rory and Angus that it was time for a pint.

There were no licensing laws in Stornoway, unlike today, except on the Sabbath when the pubs stayed closed until after the morning religious services. But if you were a visitor and knew the right door to knock on, you could have a drink whilst you were waiting for the bar to open! Rory found that if you were big enough and had money, you could drink. He followed the Scottish drinking culture consisting of the principle that if someone buys you a drink, then you must buy them one back.

A pub crawl ensued around the harbour bars, packed with sailors and townspeople and fortunately for Rory, most of them knew Captain Roddy and were buying him a drink and he was buying them one back. Not being used to drinking, Rory and Angus were five to one behind the Captain, whose sea legs were holding it well. By the time

---

23 Clinker-built where the edges of hull planks overlap.

that they reached the Anchor Tavern, Rory and Angus were way past the laughing stage, and well on the way to destination drunk.

After Rory bought a round of three pints of Old Shipwreck, a dark treacly sweet porter of 13.7% ABV (Alcohol by Volume), they all were well and truly ship-wrecked!

CHAPTER 8

Swords

Rory learned a few sea shanties[24] on the stagger back to the castle, as Angus holding the left arm of the Captain, and Rory holding the right arm, walked with three steps forward and one step back. They wound their way through the streets of Stornoway and back over the bridge, where an ice-cold reception awaited them from Lee Chan, who put her husband to bed. Rory and Angus thought that bed was a great idea, and they passed out on top of theirs whilst still fully clothed.

Both Rory and Angus felt a bit rough as they went to the morning practice the next day, and the Captain didn't look too clever either, as Lee Chan punished them for their behaviour the previous day, with a gruelling work-out. After being sick and drinking a few glasses of water they resumed the session until Lee Chan deemed them fit enough for breakfast. They were by then, totally sober, and restored to an approximation of good health. The nip from the hip flask of whisky that the Captain kept concealed from Lee Chan, took them the rest of the way.

The Captain intimated to Rory and Angus that they were going on a trip to the Clan quarry on the mountain Roineabhal on the Isle of Harris. He described that

---

24 Sea related rude songs.

the landscape there had an alien other-world look to it, with the rock being composed of anorthosite and it was similar in composition to rocks found on the mountains of the Moon. The quarry mined iron ore, and the lump graphite found in the fissure veins and fractures in the rock, which was rich in sulphur and saltpetre (Potassium Nitrate) which was used to make gunpowder when mixed with charcoal.

Rory was very interested in this, and his photographic memory recalled the picture in the book of Saint Columba of him in just such an alien environment. He knew that the time must be getting very close for him to remake his sword.

He asked the Captain and Lee Chan who knew the most about swords, and what the best way to fix a broken one was. Lee Chan and Esther's faces lit up, and they began speaking quickly to one another in Mandarin. Rory was paying a great deal of attention every time they spoke, and he was pretty sure that he understood what was being said. This was confirmed when Esther said that her Uncle Bruce at Dunscaith Castle was an expert, and had made her a samurai sword, but that she and her mum knew what was needed to fix metal. Rory asked if they would look at his broken sword, so that he could look for the right material to fix it at the quarry. Both Esther and Lee Chan agreed, and Esther went to fetch her sword for Rory to see, as he went to fetch his.

The breakfast table was cleared of the dirty dishes and Rory removed his sword from the crimson cloth, comprising a red robe, which was wrapped around it, and put all the bits of it on the table. Lee Chan and Esther were very interested in it, and examined each piece, talking to each another in Mandarin, and to Rory in English, explaining the composition of his sword to him, which they said was very strong, and that it would have taken a great deal of force to break it.

Rory asked them if they knew what would fix it, and another heated discussion took place in Mandarin, in which Rory understood words which he translated as meaning falling from the sky, but he thought that he must have got it wrong. Esther translated into English that only a special type of iron called Cliftonite, which had small graphitic crystals, would fix it, but that it was very rare as it was only found in meteoritic iron, which fell from the sky.

Rory thanked them and he re-wrapped his sword in the red robe, as Esther showed him her slightly curved rapier-like sword in its hard sheath. As she pulled it out the sheath it hissed like a snake, and Esther handled it with such grace and delicate movement that it looked as if it was an extension of her arm. This sword was being given a level of respect that Rory had not seen before by even the most skilled swordsmen at Urquhart Castle, and it looked like no sword he had ever seen before.

The Captain and Angus knew what was coming, and they moved as far away from Esther as possible, to the other side of the kitchen. Esther emitted a sweet humorous laugh as she gave them a fake scolding look, and handed Rory a long length of silk. She asked Rory to hold it up in the air in front of him and warned him not to move, especially his outstretched right arm. He did as he was told as there was a serious commanding tone to her voice, and he didn't know what to expect.

Esther took a step back, holding the straight black hilt of the sword with both hands over her head, and pointing the point of the sword to the ground behind her. With a blur of speed that Rory only vaguely saw, Esther was standing in front of him pointing the sword to the sky as he held a short piece of silk, as the rest of it floated to the ground. Angus and the Captain started clapping and then laughing, at the look of shock and comprehension on Rory's face. There were very few swords in the world that could cleanly cut silk like that, and Rory was going to meet Uncle Bruce the man who had made it!

If anyone could fix his sword he could!

It was arranged to uplift two large sturdy carts and horses from the stables in the town, that were being loaded with supplies, including many small wooden casks for the quarry, and camping gear, should it be required. The quarry men would load the carts with the return load of minerals, ore and sulphur, on their arrival after the supplies were unloaded.

Rory and Angus would take the cart loaded with the wooden casks, with the Captain and Esther taking the other, with the food and drink supplies; including a generous amount of whisky. Rory did not want to leave his sword at the castle after previously losing the Hagpipe, especially as the left tusk of the first Haggis, was used in the construction of the grip of the sword. It was very special, and he was not going to let it out of his sight, even in its broken state. Its very valuable ivory tusk grip was irreplaceable, and he had a very strange feeling that it was very important that he took it with him.

The Scottish summer was still holding sunshine and white clouds as they all set off from the green fertile farming belt around Stornoway. As they travelled south it changed to marsh lands and broken areas, with small lochs and then it changed again with mountains on the skyline to their left. It would take two days to reach the quarry on the adjoining Island of Harris, via the causeway between Lewis and Harris, and up the mountain road to Roineabhal. They relaxed into a holiday mood of travelling, pulling the heavy load and exchanging cart buddies for fresh conversations to pass the time of day.

On one exchange, Rory drove the second cart and was joined by Esther, as Angus sat with his future father-in-law, getting to know him better. This was the opportunity that Rory was waiting for, as they started off after a short break. He let Esther speak to him in English and surprised her by replying in Mandarin. Her face was a picture of surprise as Rory showed off his natural gift for languages. He only needed a few grammar tweaks from Esther, who could not believe that he had picked up her language in a few days.

They chatted away in Mandarin and Esther told him of her family's history that had been passed down from one generation to the next. The first Lee Chan was a Shaolin Monk and came to Scotland in 1291, following the Shaolin Temple being ransacked by bandits. Their monastery had been destroyed with the monks driven off or killed. He had made his way along the Silk Road[25] to Acre, where he was befriended by a Scotsman, who gave him the name Bruce. The fortress there was being attacked by a massive invading Muslim Army, and being a Buddhist, he was not safe from them, and he fought with the Scotsman to defend it.

The story goes that they both escaped by ship to protect a mythical treasure that they possessed, to keep it from this invading army. They eventually returned to Scotland where her ancestor settled at Dunscaith Castle on Skye, and married a Jacqueline MacDonald. He taught his daughter Jacqui (Jackie) Chan, whom her Mother was named after for his fighting skills, and she became known as Scáthach the Warrior Maiden.[26]

Scáthach later married Angus Og MacDonald, who was the cousin of the Lord of Skye at that time. She had a son James, who grew up, married and had a daughter Esther, who she was named after. She was the mother of her Uncle Bruce Lee Chan MacDonald and her Mum Lee Chan MacDonald. Mum married Captain Roddy MacLeod and she was the result and she smiled.

That was some story, Rory thought, and it made him think of a picture that he had seen in the book of Saint Columba of an older self, with a small man in pyjamas, who he now recognised as being Chinese, in a strange burnt

---

25 Main Trade route from China in the East to the West.
26 Translation of Scáthach means Shadow/Scatterer, due to her whirlwind fighting skills and her ability to move undetected like a shadow about the castle.

land. That must be the father of Scáthach and he must be the Scotsman who rescues him. 'This time travel thing was getting complicated,' he thought, and this couldn't be a coincidence, but what was it all about and what is this treasure?

They continued on their journey to the quarry, approaching the town of Tarbet set in the low point between the Isle of Lewis and Harris, where they would lodge in an Inn, overnight. Rory had a very strange feeling that he was being watched, but the landscape they were passing through, was bleak with no hiding places. Rory looked everywhere around him, and then looked up.

High in the sky above him was a large dark shape.[27] It had to be Ben the Eagle, keeping an eye on him with his super eagle eyes. 'He had probably been watching him since he had found him on the ship to Stornoway,' Rory thought. Well it was nice to know that he had air support (protection), but without the Hagpipe he couldn't communicate with him.

The Tarbet Inn had stables at the rear, where their horses were fed and attended to and the carts and the supplies were locked up in an outhouse. This was a regular stop on the route to the Quarry, and Captain Roddy was well known to the proprietor who, Rory noticed, welcomed him with one of those funny two-handed shakes. Angus got the same greeting with Esther and Rory only got a nod of the head as acknowledgement.

---

27 It was about the size of a modern short haul passenger plane to our eyes with flapping wings.

Rory would just have to be patient until he was sixteen, to find out what was going on. Esther was given her own bedroom above the Inn, while Roddy, Angus and Rory all shared a large room with separate beds. Angus and Esther might be engaged but the Captain was determined that they were not going to be left alone. The highland hospitality was soon flowing, easing the muscle pains from the shoogling (rocking wobbly movement) of the cart ride with a roast meat dinner all paid for by the Captain, and free drinks from the Inn Owner.

They were all up at the break of another glorious dawn and dressed for summer, with a full Scottish fry up in their bellies. This helped soothe the thumping sore heads of Angus and Rory, from the local whisky imbibed the night before, as the horses and the carts were made ready by the stable boys. The Captain seemed immune to the copious quantities of hospitality he had accepted, and was literally in high spirits. He spoke with Angus about stopping in Tarbet on the return trip, where they would be visiting the Local Lodge. Both were sharing some private joke with the inn owner that Rory and Esther were not privy to.

They resumed their journey with Rory and Angus taking the second cart with the small barrels, and Esther taking the reins of the first cart, giving her Dad a rest; who lay in the back between the supplies, taking in the morning sunshine. Rory and Angus looked at one another and both thought the same thing; that he was not as immune to the effects of whisky as he made out!

The route took them towards the rocky treacherous mountainous coastal Golden Road on Harris, which had a beautiful scattering of small lochs on either side of the road, and along it to the small village of Finsbay. They crossed over many small causeways between the lochs and up the mountain road towards the quarry. It was late afternoon when they turned a corner and saw the huge crater on their left, gouged into the mountain of Roineabhal with its strange anthracite rock. 'Take away the vegetation growing on it and you could very well be standing on the moon,' Rory thought, so barren was the landscape.

Rory heard a rattling noise coming from below the seat of the cart, where he had hidden his sword. The closer that they got to the crater the louder it became. He tried to cover up the noise and he told Angus that he would have to check the wagon springs when they stopped, in case they were getting ready to break. The open quarry was set in a half circle on the far side of the mountainside. As they approached, they saw a tented camp that was set up adjacent to the roadway, with a stone built round powder house, with a stone roof on the opposite side of the crater, as far from the camp and quarry as possible with a stone path leading up to it.

The party stopped at the tented village where a group of dirty grubby quarry men greeted the captain warmly. One of them a big burly man approached Rory and Angus and asked them to remove any personal possessions from the cart, as he was taking it to the powder house. They didn't understand what was happening, but they were glad to get their numb backsides off the cart and quickly obliged.

As Rory took hold of his wrapped broken sword from below the cart seat, he felt it vibrating in his hand. He concealed this from his companions, muffling it in the robe, not wanting them to know how special this sword really was, but something strange was happening. As he moved the sword from side to side he felt it vibrate stronger as he pointed it towards the crater, and weaker as he pointed it away.

The quarry man walked the horses and cart along the path towards the powder house where he carefully unloaded the wooden casks into it. Rory heard the head quarry man who was not as dirty as the rest, talking to the captain saying, "You just arrived in time, we had run out."

He directed one of his men to take the last of his wooden barrels to the far end of the quarry where he placed it into a prepared hole in the side of the crater at the rock face and lit a long fuse protruding from the end of the barrel. He then ran as fast as he could towards Rory and all his companions and the assembled quarry men shouted, "Fire in the hole." All the quarry men, the captain and Esther took cover behind rocks and the cart, with two of the quarry men putting a padded blanket over the horse's heads, keeping a firm hold on them.

Rory and Angus stood bewildered, wondering what was happening until they were roughly pulled behind a boulder by the Captain to join Esther. There was an almighty bang and the air was filled with dust and rocks. Rory looked up from behind the boulder to see a section of the crater and rock face collapse forward, exposing a rich vein of minerals and ore on the remaining surface of the mountain. Rory was amazed at the destructive power contained in just one small wooden barrel of gunpowder. He now realised that the Captain had him and Angus driving a cart over bumpy ground containing hundreds of these small barrels! That explains why he had kept so far in front of him on the way here, not just because he was carrying a lighter load.

Captain Roddy saw the look on Rory's face and he knew that it had dawned on him what the load was, that he had been transporting. He gave a loud laugh and slapped Rory on the back. Everyone got up from behind their protected places and walked towards the new blast hole to examine the treasures that it might reveal.

Rory followed them, still carrying his sword. The further he walked through the crater, the harder the sword vibrated in his hands. Fortunately, everyone was in front of him as the top half of the broken sword with the hilt and carved Nessie handle made from the left tusk of the first Haggis, pulled free from the red robe covering it.

It flew through the air and embedded itself in the new pile of rocks and dust in front of him. Rory hurried to where the sword was buried up to the hilt in the ground and frantically dug at the earth with his hands, to retrieve the sword. He pulled at it and it gave way, attached to a very heavy shiny black sparkling palm-sized rock. It was stuck fast, like a strong magnet to the broken shaft of the sword. It was Meteoric Cliftonite,[28] which had been buried when the crater had been created by a meteor strike. The explosion had released it from the quarry face, and

---

28 Iron containing graphite crystals

the sword had sought out and found the very element that it needed to be remade!

No one was aware of these events behind them, as Rory quickly re-wrapped his sword and the stone of Cliftonite in the robe, along with the smaller pieces, which had all moved together to join the main part, and had stuck solid to the rock.

The pieces could not be separated from it, no matter how hard Rory pulled at them, and he was definitely not going to lose any. None of this was seen by anyone else. The attention of Captain Roddy, Angus, Esther and all the quarry men, was on the rock face, and the shining vein in front of them.

The Macleod's had just struck gold!

CHAPTER 9

Dunscaith

It was a very happy Captain Roddy on the return trip to Stornoway, with two full carts of iron ore, saltpetre, sulphur and gold. The road was smoother, if not slightly longer as they carried on around the mountain of Roineabhal, towards Leverburgh where the ferry crossing to the Isle of Uist was situated. They travelled through the flat fertile farming ground of Harris, which was fed with seaweed, producing bumper crops of wheat and barley. They arrived back at the Tarbet Inn where Rory was left with Esther, as Angus and Captain Roddy joined the Innkeeper on their arranged visit to the Tarbet Lodge.

Rory too could have secrets, as he showed Esther the Cliftonite stuck to the sword and told her the story of it. Esther was not dismissive in any way, and believed all that Rory had said. She said that a sword like his was owned by the Scotsman who had rescued her ancestor, and was said to be magical. Rory deflected her next question on where he had got it from, by saying it was an heirloom that had been passed down to him, which was basically true. She said that she was sure that her uncle Bruce would be very happy to give Rory any assistance possible, to remake the sword. They spoke for hours until the returning visiting drunks staggered in and were aided to their beds by Rory and Esther.

The next morning the journey home continued, with the weather staying fine, as both Angus and the Captain dozed on top of the lumpy load in the back of the carts. They had a short stop on the way back at the Weavers in Luskentyre, where the famous Harris Tweed was made. It was situated overlooking Luskentyre beach and the Island of Taransay, which was the most beautiful place that Rory had ever seen.

The miles of golden white sand were far too tempting for him, and it lured him to it as if a spell had been cast on him. The Captain had business to purchase a supply of tweed from the owner Donald John MacKay, who he had met on his last visit to the Tarbet Lodge. They had eaten Stornoway black pudding, and had drunk whisky together, and were on good terms, but business was business.

Rory stripped off his socks and his sandals and went for a paddle in the sea, where he saw two huge basking sharks filtering the plankton -rich blue waters, between the beach and the small Island of Taransay. He was joined by Esther and Angus, and all three laughed and splashed about, enjoying the sunshine, the sand and their first beach holiday.

After a short while, they joined the Captain who was being served tea and biscuits in Donald's kitchen. Rory was sure that he could smell whisky from the Captains tea, which was confirmed when he spotted a cold stare from Esther directed at her Dad. He defended himself, and stated that it was just a wee hair of the dog.[29]

---

29 The meaning is that you take a bit more of the same poison that had bitten you the night before to cure your ills. In this case the Whisky.

The rest of the journey back was uneventful, but Rory was sure that he had spotted Ben the Eagle high in the sky, still watching him. They followed the western flat coastal route back to minimize damage to the suspension of the carts, due to the heavy load that they were carrying.

As they approached Callanish a huge standing stone circle appeared on the hillside on their left. Rory felt a shiver as if someone had just walked over his grave, as he had heard a high-pitched squeal. He looked about, but none of his other companions appeared to feel or notice anything. He looked towards the standing stones and he saw a shimmering emit from the ground in a perfect circle, straight up into the sky, disappearing from sight into the heavens.

At this time, he heard another noise and a squawking squeal replying to the first one, which he recognised as belonging to Ben. He watched the sky and he saw Ben flying at full speed towards the centre of the standing stones and into the shimmering beam, where he vanished, along with the shimmer, as he entered it. He could travel through time as well, Rory thought, by using the standing stones.

He felt that Ben had been called with the first squeal, which he now recognised as being the squeal of the Hagpipe. Rory had felt for a few seconds when the portal was open, that he was in grave danger. It was as if a future self had the Hagpipe back, and had used it to open a portal, and that he faced a great danger, perhaps even death. He was sure that Ben would save himself, as this was the call that he appeared to be waiting for.

He would have to wait to find out what had happened, as he had inadvertently guided Ben who had followed him to the standing stones to receive this call. Rory was quite shaken by this realisation, and he went white in the face at the way that these events were being woven together.

Angus noticed this and asked him if he was okay. Rory nodded. No one else had even noticed what had happened!

On arrival back in Stornoway, the carts were left at the stables to be unloaded, except for the bag of gold, that was kept tight in the Captains grasp. He was desperate to show it to his brother the Lord of the Isles of Lewis and Harris, Torquil MacLeod. This discovery was going to make him very rich and even more powerful.

It was planned to have a few weeks rest and then to sail down to Dunscaith Castle on the Isle of Skye, for the wedding of Angus and Esther on September the twenty sixth. Esther was very excited about her final fitting for her wedding dress which was being made by the head seamstress of the castle. A new dress kilt awaited Angus at Dunscaith, but he couldn't comprehend all the dizzy excitement shown by Esther. The Captain was very happy and had he had arranged for a trusted Clansman to travel to the quarry, to oversee the mining of the gold. He had plenty of time on his hands now, to spend with Angus in the local pubs. He considered him a good omen, after the discovery of the gold and he fully accepted him into the family as a new son.

Rory took the opportunity to spend some of his money in the town, buying a new dress kilt and to look for a wedding present for Angus and Esther. He decided on an ornate sturdy dining table and chairs, which he arranged to be packed and loaded aboard the Stag, for the short trip back to Dunscaith. Angus had asked him to be his best man, which made Rory very happy, and this called for a good wedding present.

The weather had changed as August gave way to September, with the distinct possibility of stormy weather, both inside and out, as the wedding party including the Lord of the Isle, Torquil MacLeod set off from Stornoway to Dunscaith.

He would be meeting the other Clan chiefs, to discuss some misunderstandings (usually involving raids and cattle stealing) between them, after the wedding. The joining of Angus and Esther further cemented the close bond between the Clans of the MacLeods and the MacDonalds, and this was the show of strength that gave both Clans a hefty advantage in discussions with the other Clans.

Dunscaith Castle was a formidable place that sat on an offshore rock forty feet above sea level, with a twenty-foot gap between the rock and the mainland, spanned by a walled bridge, with arches six foot apart. The bridge led onto a drawbridge, which opened onto a flight of stairs, between by two walls, which led up to the castle and the inner buildings. A central well was in the courtyard, next to a tall watchtower. If you did get in uninvited you definitely didn't get out.

Next to the castle was a secluded secure bay, where the MacDonald fleet of Galleys was harboured. Security was very tight regarding all the visitors to the castle. If you were not vouched for you, were going nowhere other than to jail, where you would stay until a name was given of a sponsor to come to your rescue.

Eoin MacDonald the Lord of the Isle of Skye, was standing on the pier, awaiting the arrival of his son Angus and the wedding party on the Stag. It had been closely watched, as it approached the castle, by the lookouts manning the observation points along the coast of Skye, following a pigeon message, which had been sent from Stornoway to Dunscaith Castle, with word of its imminent arrival. The ship, as a result, was expected. If this message had not been received or it may not have made it, it could have been intercepted by a war galley or sunk by a cannon shot from the coast.

The wedding party was warmly welcomed with the two Lords of the Isles, Torquil MacLeod and Eoin MacDonald exchanging warm greetings and two-handed shakes. The rest of the wedding party followed the VIP's to the castle, for a lavish reception and left the crew and the MacDonald guards to unload the ship.

Rory felt intimidated by the security and the defences of Dunscaith and he was glad that he was a friend and not a foe. The castle looked poor and ancient from the outside but was lavish and opulent on the inside, with its great hall hung with full length tapestries depicting the history of Clan MacDonald. Stag heads and other trophies were fixed to the wall above the top table, which had silver jugs and cups as standard tableware.

Large silver salvers of mixed cooked meats and fresh bread adorned the large top table where they were seated, with the two lords at the top seated together. Well, Rory thought he wasn't going to starve and if this was just a snack what was the wedding feast going to be like. After they were fully sated Angus took Rory on a guided tour of the castle, whilst Esther and her mum Lee Chan, went to visit her brother Bruce Lee Mac Donald and his family, leaving the two lords and Captain Roddy talking and drinking.

The castle was a rabbit warren of passages and staircases that seemed to double back on themselves, and Rory was sure that without the guidance of Angus, he would be totally lost, as he took him to a remote unused part of the castle. It was in a large blank heavy stone room, where they were going to set up a modern foundry with an improved design, but it was similar to the high heat one at Urquhart Castle. Rory recognised this room immediately, although he had never been there before. It was the room he had seen in the book of Saint Columba, where he had remade the sword. The events in the book were coming true again!

Preparations had already begun for the construction of the new forge, with an adjacent storeroom full of various sized anvils and hammers and a large oversized bellows which would require two strong men to pump. This would be essential to make sure that the fire was hot enough, as the melting point of iron was much higher than that of bronze.

The new forge was also close to the castle's well, as large quantities of clean water to cool the metal were also required. A large quantity of charcoal, free of the impurities of sulphur was also stacked in sacks against the storeroom wall. This would make the fire hot enough to melt iron. Someone had anticipated the requirements of the new forge, with the basics already in place, awaiting the assembly of all the parts. Angus smiled and he was pleased at what he could see, and he knew that all the hard work had been done already.

Only one person here had this level of knowledge of the techniques of smelting, forging and tempering the metal. These were a family and trade secrets, and the possessor of them had silently walked into the room behind them.

Bruce Lee Chan MacLeod was in his mid-fifties, but looked twenty years younger than that, due to retaining his ancestral genetic Asian features. He was five feet eight inches tall, and slim built below his loose-fitting blue cotton tunic and trousers. He saw the look of surprise on the faces of Rory and Angus, as they turned and saw him standing behind them, and he smiled warmly, with his clean-shaven face and his bald head, with a long grey black pleated pony tail dangling behind his head.

Rory recognised him!

He was identical to the picture in the book of Saint Columba from ACRE, and the rescue of the treasure. Rory greeted him warmly in Mandarin, and it was Angus and Rory's turn to smile at the look of surprise on his face. An understanding was quickly achieved between Rory and Bruce, as they bowed to one another, not breaking eye contact and not underestimating one another.

They spoke of the plans for the new forge, exchanging their knowledge of gun making and techniques. All three of them were surprised at one another, as they demonstrated their experience and their knowledge on how to improve the forge. This would be the most modern and the most efficient forge of its time, and over the next week, it was built by the three of them together, all speaking in Mandarin and becoming the best of friends.

The twenty sixth of September came with the first great storm of the oncoming winter, battering the castle from the Atlantic Ocean. The weather did not affect life inside the castle which had been built to withstand these conditions, which went on as normal. Rory settled into a routine, up at dawn with Randori practice, in a similar room as in Stornoway Castle, with Angus, Esther, the Captain, Lee Chan and her brother Bruce, and his children, young Bruce and his sister Jacqui, who were the same age as Rory and Esther.

Young Bruce was slight built, like his Dad, with a wiry strong frame. Jacqui was slightly smaller than Esther but could pass as her twin sister, not her cousin. The only family member not taking part was Martha, the wife of Bruce and the sister of Eoin MacDonald the lord of the Isle of Skye, the father of Angus. She was a formidable well-made woman about five feet six inches tall, with greying dark shoulder-length hair. She said that she did not need to know self-defence. One word from her, and you did what you were told, and no one was brave or foolish enough to disagree with her. Her voice was her weapon, and there was no defence from that! Bruce compared Martha to a Chinese dragon, as he spoke to Rory, and all the family agreed with him with much hilarity. But they made sure that they were well out of earshot of Martha, as they spoke in Mandarin about her, which she said she could not understand, just in case she could!

The classes were always taken jointly by Bruce and Lee Chan, who Rory quickly realised, had equal skills when he saw them fighting together. No one else shared the mat with them and everyone kept well out of their way. There was a lot of Brotherly/Sisterly love between them! They had been brought up practising together as children, and they still tried to prove who was the best, with no holds barred. Rory watched in awe when they fought, and he knew that it would take him years if not forever, to have that level of skill and speed.

A special wedding breakfast followed the practice with all the family and Rory sitting, eating and talking together. You could cut the excitement with a knife, between Esther and her bridesmaid Jacqui, who constantly chattered to one another, with no time or inclination to eat. Final preparations for the wedding came after breakfast, with the head Abbot from Iona who had arrived to conduct this important ceremony. Martha was in charge, and she was accompanied by Esther and Jackie. Martha was like a surrogate mother-in-law to Esther, following the death of Angus's mother, when he was born.

Martha had helped to raise Angus and she was more like a mother to him than an aunt. Martha was in charge, and it took a lot of persuasion from her husband Bruce and Angus, for her to relinquish any control of the wedding arrangements to Esther.

The Head Abbot of Iona Abbey, Ian Campbell the second (Gaelic Eóin Caimbeul II), had travelled to Dunscaith a few days before to conduct the wedding, and the castle was now bristling with rich guests, laden with silverware and expensive gifts for the happy couple, but more so, to show their own importance to their peers.

The MacLeod's and the MacDonald's had a long history with Iona Abbey, and their current Lords had been inducted and then buried there for generations. Abbot Ian Campbell was a slim man, with a round face in his middle sixties; about five-foot nine inches in height, with a bald head with short grey hair at the sides. He was similarly dressed as the Abbot of Urquhart Castle, but was wearing a purple monk's habit, denoting his rank.

He carried a long wooden crosier (staff), which was ornately carved with crosses. He had passed the book of Saint Columba to Abbot Malcolm MacCallum, following the instructions in its index, when he had left Iona to take up his position at Urquhart Castle.

The book had shown him his preordained time to meet Rory, which was quickly approaching. The large left tusk of the first Haggis, which Rory had unknowingly recovered from the pile in the Haggis graveyard, had been meticulously carved by Abbot MacCallum into the curved shape of Nessie. It had been made for the grip on Rory's Sword which was non-slip, because of the three humps on the back and two antennas on the head of Nessie which fitted perfectly with Rory's two-handed grip on the Sword.

He had received the "new" Sword Grip from Abbot MacCallum by courier, and the time was drawing close for the Sword to be remade, and for him to give Rory this

Haggis Tusk Sword Grip. Something special was going to happen, and he looked forward to being a part of it.

Rory had shown his broken Sword to Bruce, which was still stuck fast to the lump of Cliftonite. Bruce said that he had made many special Swords, but he had never seen one like this. In his opinion it was magical, and he would be proud to assist in its remaking. The new forge was finished, and they planned that the Sword would be the first work to be carried out in it when it was lit, following the wedding. Bruce said that this would bring the forge luck if they successfully remade it. They could not even consider failure!

The whole castle was bustling with servants, running about and the main kitchen was in full swing, preparing the various courses for the wedding feast, starting with Cullen Skink, a special fish soup, to fresh Scallops and Prawns, to a full roast hog and venison, and a variety of other meats, with assorted vegetables and tatties (potatoes).

The great hall was decked out, cloth coverings were over the chairs and tables, with a careful seating plan, put in place to avoid having feuding Clans from sitting next to one another. The Head Abbot was going to conduct the wedding in the great hall, as it was the only room large enough to fit in all the visiting dignitaries and guests. A central aisle had been left through the middle of the room, for the bride and her father, proud Roddy, who was to walk her down the aisle to give her away to her new husband.

All the men and the boys had been banished to Bruce and Martha's quarters, to get ready for the wedding. Esther and her Mum Lee Chan and bridesmaid Jacqui and new surrogate mother-in-law Martha, had moved into the suite of the Lord of the Isles of Skye. Eoin had not resided in the rooms since the death of Angus's Mum. He prefers to live in single quarters near to the great hall, as he said that they had too many bad memories for him. The suite had been lavishly restored, and was now the living quarters of the future Lord and Lady of the Isle, and hopefully their family.

The table and chairs that Rory had bought had been delivered and they took pride of place in their private dining room. Esther blushed, and Jackie giggled when she saw the huge four poster bed, a present from her new father-in-law in the master bedroom. Only Esther, Lee Chan, Jacqui and Martha were allowed to see the wedding dress, prior to the wedding, as it was considered bad luck for the groom to see her in it. Martha smiled as she was enjoying herself, which was a rare occurrence as all three were pampered by the servants, getting their hair done and dressed in their matching bridesmaid dresses, designed by Martha to complement the wedding dress.

The men and the boys equally enjoyed themselves sharing a wee dram of Dutch courage, as they made themselves presentable in their best dress kilts. Roddy was dressed first and he went off to make sure that Esther was not going to be late for the wedding. Eoin Lord of Skye and Torquil Lord of Lewis, accompanied by Angus, Rory and Faither (Father) and Junior Bruce, headed towards the Great Hall. Rory stood next to Angus with their backs to the aisle, awaiting the bride. Eoin and Torquil were bonding their special relationship with rare fine whisky, and they went together to join the other Clan Leaders. They enjoyed the looks from them, and they listened to the whispered comments as they passed, at their obvious friendship.

Rory was twitchy, as he was in charge of the two matching gold wedding rings supplied by Torquil MacLeod, made from the first batch of gold from his new gold mine.

Everyone besides Eoin and Torquil was nervous for different reasons. Rory was scared that he would lose the rings and of the speech he had to make. Angus stood with his knees knocking together at the prospect of getting married, and the rival Clan Chiefs were nervous at the power battle unfolding in front of them, and wondering who would snap first.

You could cut the tension with a knife as the ceilidh band started to play the wedding march, and a very proud Roddy MacLeod walked in with his stunning daughter, all dressed in white, in her delicate lace embroidered wedding dress and veil and a long train held by Jacqui. She and Lee Chan and Martha all matched, dressed in pink lace dresses and they turned a few heads themselves, and they thoroughly enjoyed all the attention. Unknown to Martha she turned heads for the wrong reason, as pink did not suit her as she resembled a bowl of wobbly pink blancmange, on legs[30].

---

30 Blancmange from French blanc-manger a sweet dessert commonly made with milk or cream and sugar thickened with gelatine, corn-starch or Irish moss.

Rory had to practically hold Angus up, as Esther came to stand alongside him, as his legs buckled on seeing her. The Head Abbot Ian Campbell started the service, to a hushed silence. The whole audience respected the Monks of Saint Columba, as though they might fall out amongst themselves, but not one of them wanted to offend him. The time came when he instructed the bridesmaid Jacqui to remove Esther's veil. She stood beaming the most beautiful smile anyone had ever seen at Angus as he stood entranced in her presence along with every other man in the room.

Angus felt the luckiest man in the world as he took his vows and said, "I do"!

CHAPTER 10

Rebirth

The speeches were over, and Rory was relaxed at not losing the rings, and only stuttering a little during his speech. He had spoken about the groom and how they first become friends as he had cleaned up his sick, after his initiation ceremony. This seemed to go down very well with a large part of the audience, who began nudging and joking with one another. A few of them came up to Rory afterwards, to congratulate him, and they shook his hand with a funny grip. They obviously thought that he was older than he was, due to his size and thought that he had passed his manhood ceremony, and so gave him a funny look when he couldn't respond.

After a short word with Angus, he saw them nod their heads and talk among themselves and they gave a conspiratorial smile to Rory, as he heard them plan to be at his initiation. Rory still didn't understand what was going on, but he was going to have to be very careful as he didn't like the look of their smiles at all.

As at all Scottish Weddings, the Bride and the Groom had the first dance, followed by the parents, swapping partners, with Eoin dancing with Lee Chan, and Roddy dancing with Martha and Rory dancing with Jacqui. Rory had to concentrate not to stand on her toes but she seemed very happy, smiling at him with a look that reminded him of the way Heather had smiled at him.

Rory felt a moment of sadness missing Heather, but Jacqui had a firm hold on him, making him speak to her. He wanted to be left alone with his thoughts, but try as he might, he could not avoid Jacqui, who kept finding him for another dance, much to the amusement of Angus and Esther.

The free bar supplied by Eoin had its effect on the guests, with a few minor fights (well no bones were broken!) as old scores were beginning to be settled by rival Clans, full of Dutch courage. Bruce did not drink alcohol, and he had volunteered to steward the wedding, but he had his work cut out keeping the peace. He was well equipped for the challenge, and he enjoyed himself separating combatants who were on the verge of becoming out of order (using a weapon).

Bruce acted as a bouncer, and anyone who stepped out of line was quickly bounced by Bruce – out the door. He watched everyone making fools of themselves and he listened carefully to their private conversations, gleaming important information amid their drunken ramblings, which he would later report back to Eoin. This would be used to increase his influence and his power with the other Clan leaders, when they met, giving him some extra leverage.

Soon some of the greedier guests were passed out, resting their heads on the tables as the Bride and the Groom left the party, to go to their new married quarters. Angus carried Esther over the threshold almost bumping her head on the door support, before they collapsed, laughing on the giant four-poster bed.

The castle was full of sore heads the next morning, as everyone tried to recall what they had said, and done the previous night, and with whom. The Wedding had been a great success and typical of all Scottish Weddings it had involved food, drink and fighting. Rory was not exempt from the over-indulgence of the previous night. It was his turn for a bucket and a jug of water beside his bed, as he passed out from all the whisky he had been 'forced' to consume.

The only person who had no ill effects, was Bruce, who refused to drink alcohol and who looked after Rory, making sure that he was all right, by nursing him back, if not to health, back to feeling that he wanted to live. He was keen to get on with the remaking of the Sword, and he was just as excited as Rory, to get the new forge fired up. He knew that there was something very special about the Sword, and that it was alive in some way, and was not just an inanimate object. He had felt that way before, when he had handled the Samurai Sword of Scáthach, made by her father, which he kept safely hidden away.

Angus and Esther had gone on a short honeymoon, travelling back to Harris on the Stag, which also returned the wedding guests to Stornoway. They were dropped off with supplies, to survive a month, never mind the two weeks at Atlantic Cottage, overlooking the beautiful beach of Luskentyre. They did not have to leave the cottage, if they did not want to.

They had been similarly bewitched, as Rory was, with Luskentyre Beach, which they had seen on their return visit from the quarry, and could not think of a more desirable place to spend time together.

Rory and Bruce fired up the new foundry and were very happy with the intense heat that it produced from the oversized bellows, feeding it oxygen. They stripped down Rory's Sword, removing the handle grip and hilt from the main part of the sword blade, which refused to be parted from the lump of Cliftonite.

The other broken pieces of the blade were still stuck solid, but they began to move as if pulled by a strong magnet, into place, as if completing a jigsaw puzzle, until they fell into place, forming the whole shape of the Long Sword. It was as if the sword wanted to help to remake itself.

Rory noticed that the left Haggis Tusk handle of the Sword carved in its Nessie shape was becoming translucent!

He had seen this before in Hag's cave as the procession of dying Haggis walked towards the Haggis graveyard, where they faded from existence, leaving their Tusks behind on the pile. He thought that this must be happening, as it was disconnected from the Sword.

They would have to work quickly before it disappeared altogether!

Bruce and Rory placed the broken pieces still stuck fast in the shape of the long sword, with the lump of Cliftonite into the forge. They pumped the huge bellows supplying a large quantity of oxygen to the charcoal fire, making it white hot.

Both watched in amazement as the Black Cliftonite melted like butter into the cracks of the blade, leaving it whole. Bruce had never seen a blade stick back together like this, and he said that it must be hammered and folded to give it its strength back. They both worked furiously, allowing it to become white hot, then they removed it and took it in turns dripping with sweat, to hammer and to fold the blade. They then cooled it in water, and repeated this process, until no trace of the crack marks where the Sword was re-joined, could be seen.

They worked so hard and they focused so much on their task that they did not see the Head Abbot of Iona Abbey Ian Campbell come into the foundry. He watched them as finally satisfied with the blade, they sharpened it on a stone file and reattached the hilt.

Rory held it up with his left hand on the middle of the blade, and he turned to the light coming in the door, to admire their work. Both Rory and Bruce saw the Abbot watching them, smiling. He put his hand inside his robe and he pulled out a cloth wrapped shape. As they watched the Abbot, they saw his smile change into one of dismay, as the cloth went flat and empty in his palm. Rory turned to the work bench and looked for the Haggis/Nessie grip. It was gone, vanished just like the Abbot's package.

They were too late!

Rory looked at Bruce and at the Abbot. His face was a picture of dismay. He had taken too long to remake the Sword. The left Tusk of the first Haggis was gone, just like the right one of the Hagpipe!

The expression on the face of the Abbot changed almost immediately, and his mouth dropped open, as he looked at Rory's left hand. He was holding the completed Long Sword shimmering and sparkling; topped with the new ivory white reborn Haggis/Nessie grip!

Bruce was taken aback at this obvious display of magic as the Abbot explained to Rory the real reason of why he was here. It was to deliver the new Haggis/Nessie grip to him. Rory was unaware until this time that he had found this tusk in Hag's cave in the mound of tusks and that it was the big one of the seven, that he had given to the Abbot of Urquhart Castle. He told Rory how he had seen his picture in the book of Saint Columba of him holding the remade Sword with his left hand, and that it was his destiny to deliver it to him.

This was one of the pictures that Rory had not been shown, as some pages were marked by Saint Columba, saying that he was not to have shown them until the event had happened.

What other pictures had he not been shown? Rory thought!

The Abbot continued, saying that even he was surprised at what had happened, and he wished Rory well to continue with the rest of his destiny. This made him wonder again at what his future held, as Abbot Campbell gave him a wry smile and left to return to Iona.

Rory had more to think about again, but he wanted to try the sword out. Bruce picked up a broadsword from a pile in for repair and they had a practice swing of both swords to judge their weight. As soon as Rory took hold of the grip on his sword with both his hands it felt like the sword was merging with his arms, becoming part of his body.

Bruce took a swing at Rory and he felt his sword move as if it had a mind of its own and Rory realised that it had anticipated the impending strike, blocking it. Bruce increased his speed and Rory countered with the same speed, until Bruce had used all his skill and was becoming exhausted, while Rory could have been sleeping for all the energy that he was expending as his sword was doing all the work.

Bruce was at the limits of all his skill and ability, and he became frustrated when he released all his restraints and went for a killer blow to Rory's body. The sword casually turned into the blow, cutting the long sword held by Bruce in half, as if it were a twig.

It went flying from his arms in two halves as the Nessie Sword finished up with its point at Bruce's throat. Both Rory and Bruce were overwhelmed. Bruce was upset at himself for losing control and for not being able to beat Rory, and more so for going in for a killing blow.

Bruce was very glad that he had been stopped!

Rory was amazed at how easily he had defended himself and he was concerned at the killer instinct that the sword had displayed, but he was relieved that he had had the final say over whether to kill Bruce or not. He was glad that he was able to exert his will to control the sword, as he didn't want to hurt Bruce, but it had been a struggle and it had taken all his resolve to stop it from killing Bruce.

The sword was very dangerous, but it had obeyed him. As a test, Rory asked Bruce to try his sword out, to see how it behaved for him and he handed it to him. Bruce took hold of it by its grip but try as he might, he could not hold it. The handle was slippery. It was like holding a bar of butter. He juggled with it, trying to hold it, but it refused him and fell out of his hands, embedding itself into the stone floor by its tip, halfway up to its hilt.

Rory extended his right hand to take hold of the Haggis/Nessie grip. The sword practically jumped from the ground into his outstretched hand, and he could easily pull it out of the stone floor.

It was if it had been stuck in soft earth, and not stone and he saw the deep, long, blade- length hole where it had been.

Both he and Bruce examined the blade. It was undamaged, with not the slightest scratch, and it shimmered almost tauntingly at them, as if to say, "You will have to do better than that!" Rory put the sword down on the nearby work bench and held out his right hand towards it again thinking 'hand'. Unrestrained, it flew through the air into his hand. Bruce was becoming very nervous now at the magic he was witnessing. Rory had suspected that the sword would act in this way like the broken one had in the quarry.

He was the strong magnetic force as the Cliftonite was to the metal, and he only had to think about it coming into his hand, and it did. Rory decided to give this living sword a name, and called it Hans, as that was what it did when he wanted it to!

He would have to be careful going by the reaction of Bruce, of its abilities, as people were very scared of anything occult and magical. This could cause him a real problem if they thought that he was involved in witch-craft, and they might turn against him.

Only Rory could handle the sword which was good, as it could never be used against him but, what on Earth had broken it previously?

CHAPTER 11

Fingal's Cave

Bruce was very wary of the power of Rory's sword and he told him so. He said that he would give him special instruction in his Kung Fu style of unarmed fighting to save him from having to use it. He had never experienced a sword that behaved in this manner before, and he said that it had a life of its own.

Rory thought that he knew what it was, it was the power of the Haggis, but he wasn't going to tell Bruce that. If the sword was as powerful as that now, how strong was he going to be if he ever got the Hagpipe back with its twin right tusk?

Rory quite fancied being able to fight as well as Bruce and Lee Chan, and he accepted Bruce's offer and slid his sword back into the hole in the foundry floor. As a test, he asked Bruce to pull the sword free. No matter how hard he pulled at the Nessie/Haggis tusk handle or hilt, his grip slipped and his hands could not take hold of it. Rory thought that there could be no safer place to keep his sword in the castle and he left it there.

This proved a great attraction over the next year and a half to the MacLeod warriors. It did not matter how big or strong they were, for when they visited the foundry to have their weapons repaired none of them could resist attempting to pull the sword from the floor. Every one failed and the myth of the 'Sword in the Stone' and the boy who could remove it, soon spread all around Scotland and further afield, thanks to the visiting gossip of a Knight called Arthur King who came to the castle a lot (Camelot).

Rory was now fifteen and he still continued to grow, adding another two inches to his previous six foot with more muscle and agility from his training with Bruce, and from the work in the foundry. Angus still worked there, but he was preoccupied with married life and he was soon going to be a father, as Esther was expecting a baby in the spring. Rory told Angus that he would stay at Dunscaith until the baby was born.

He told him that he had promised to go back to Urquhart Castle for his birthday and manhood ceremony, on the twenty fourth of June.

The baby was due at the end of February or at the beginning of March. Angus said that he, Esther and the baby would like to join him on his trip, as they could do with a holiday and he wanted to be there for Rory's Initiation.

March came and much to the relief of all, but especially Angus and his dad Eoin, he became a father and grandfather of a bouncing eight-pound boy on the second day of the new month. He had jet black hair, just like his Mum. A pigeon was sent to Stornoway and it was arranged for Esther's Mum and Dad to travel back to Dunscaith Castle on the Stag, for the christening of two-month-old Eoin Roderick MacLeod, on the eighth of May. Both Eoin and Captain Roddy were very proud grandparents, with their first grandchild named after them.

Abbot Ian Campbell had been contacted at Iona Abbey and he would come to perform the Christening. Captain Roddy would then take him back to Iona, along with Angus, Esther, Lee Chan, Rory and baby Eoin, where he would be further blessed. The Stag would then cruise down the West Coast, and up the channel to Fort William, where Rory, Angus and Esther and the baby would disembark and travel overland back to Urquhart Castle.

Captain Roddy would then return to Stornoway with his wife, and sail back around the coast and down Loch Ness to Urquhart Castle, in time for Rory's Initiation and a reunion with their grandchild.

The christening was a family affair, held in the small chapel in Dunscaith. Baby Eoin behaved; impeccably dressed in the MacLeod family shawl and he didn't cry as his head was anointed with holy water. The adults then did some anointing themselves with the best whisky Granddad Eoin had maturing in his cellar!

The next day after a sobering breakfast, Captain Roddy joined Rory and Angus on a visit to the foundry, to recover the sword for their trip to Urquhart Castle. Roddy had heard of this famed 'Sword in the Stone' and had to see it for himself. He pulled at it until he was red in the face, and he fell backwards, landing on his backside. Both Rory and Angus laughed, and he was convinced that it was a trick, when Rory easily pulled it free with his left hand.

Rory placed the sword in a long leather sheath, which was placed on his back in warrior style, and was held on with two straps of leather under each arm. This gave easy access to the grip at the top, when reaching overhead with both hands.

The christening party, accompanied by Abbot Campbell, boarded the Stag on a crisp fresh spring May morning. They were waved off by all the family and friends from the castle, including Bruce and Martha.

Bruce was pleased to see the sword out of his foundry floor, but he didn't know what to do with the hole it had left, so he considered it a sign of good luck. An emotional Lord of Skye- Eoin, was unhappy at the imminent departure of his grandson, and an even more emotional Jackie was crying at the departure of Rory. What was it with him leaving on boats, that made girls cry? Rory thought!

Captain Roddy took charge of the Stag for its short sail down to Iona. Abbot Ian Campbell wanted to make a short stop in the Holy Cave, on the Isle of Staffa, to conduct a special blessing in the cathedral-like cave on the future Lord of the Isle of Skye, baby Eoin. The Holy Cave was very special and it faced towards the Isle of Iona, and it is well known today by the name 'Fingal's Cave'[31].

---

31 Fingal's Cave is a sea cave on the uninhabited island of Staffa, in the Inner Hebrides of Scotland. It is known for its natural acoustics. The cave's Gaelic name, An Uaimh Bhinn means "the melodious cave". The National Trust for Scotland owns the cave, as part of a National Nature Reserve. It became known as Fingal's Cave after the eponymous hero of an epic poem by eighteenth-century Scots poet-historian James Macpherson. Excerpt from Wikipedia.

The cave's size and naturally arched roof produced eerie sounds, reportedly caused by the echoes of waves, which gave it the atmosphere of a natural cathedral. The local farming and fishing population residing on the part of Iona facing the cave on Staffa, frequently heard these eerie sounds coming across the sea. It was rumoured by them that the sounds were made by a sea beast, looking for its master and some even reported seeing the head of the beast sticking out of the sea.

This caused some ridicule from the other residents and anyone spotting the monster usually kept the fact to themselves!

Captain Roddy sailed the Stag towards Staffa and all the crew and the passengers were on the deck, to see the prehistoric Island as it came into view.

Roddy ordered the sails lowered and the crew to man the oars, as the Stag was manoeuvred into the deep channel leading to the main cathedral cave and berthed at the natural rocky shelved pier to gasps of wonder at the beauty of the cave's interior[32].

The christening party led by Captain Roddy and Abbot Ian Campbell disembarked onto a level wide rocky shelf and were followed by the awestruck father Angus and his wife Esther. The care of baby Eoin was delegated to the sure grasp of Granny Lee Chan, who was very sure of her footing, as she disembarked the ship, followed by Rory, onto the slippery rocky steps of Fingal's Cave. Every noise they made echoed around the cave, along with the noise of the waves lapping against the interior rocky walls.

Everyone was amazed at the cave, even the Abbot, who had visited it several times. The basaltic pillars were as high as the roof of a cathedral, with the deep and swelling sea eternally running deep into the rock.

---

32 Fingal's Cave is formed entirely from hexagonally jointed basalt columns within a Palaeocene lava flow, similar in structure to the Giant's Causeway in Northern Ireland. In all these cases, cooling on the upper and lower surfaces of the solidified lava resulted in contraction and fracturing, starting in a blocky tetragonal pattern and transitioning to a regular hexagonal fracture pattern with fractures perpendicular to the cooling surfaces. As cooling continued these cracks gradually extended toward the centre of the flow, forming the long hexagonal columns we see in the wave-eroded cross-section today. Excerpt from Wikipedia.

The square raised paved ground looked like ruddy marble, and the look of it baffled all description. It was truly a wonder of the world, dating back to the volcanic creation of the Island.

Lee Chan passed baby Eoin to Esther, who, in turn, handed him to Abbot Campbell. Everyone fell silent as he held baby Eoin up towards the golden shimmering roof, as he praised God and blessed him in his name, as his voice echoed around the cave, repeating the blessing back several times.

If you did not believe in God, you would do so by the end of this blessing in this theatre of His work. Shivers ran down the backs of all those present, who had witnessed and had heard the vibrations of the Abbot's voice, mixed with the natural noises of the cave, as they radiated around them. Baby Eoin was totally silent until the echoes stopped, and then he let out a deafening cry that shook and rattled off the walls, and struck him dumb, as it returned to him.

Everyone laughed at the look of shock on his face, as if to say, "Did I do that?" The laughter was still echoing around the cave as they all re-boarded the Stag, which was rowed out of the cave back to the sea. The ship had just turned to face Iona, to finish the short crossing to it, with the sails being raised, when Rory heard a loud eerie squeal that came from Fingal's Cave.

Rory rushed to the rear of the Stag, along with Angus and Esther as Lee Chan held baby Eoin on the upper deck with Captain Roddy. All three of them watched as the entrance to Fingal's Cave shimmered and a huge grey/ blue monster with a long flexible neck and three humps on its back, powered out of the cave propelled by its four diamond-shaped flippers.

It was Nessie! 'The cry of baby Eoin have must have got her attention,' Rory thought. That means that Fingal's Cave is a portal to Loch Ness and connected by the Lay Lines. That is why she is not always in the Loch, as she has access to the open sea!

Nessie saw the Stag and she started to swim towards the ship. How could Rory explain himself to everyone when Nessie swam up to him, wanting a tickle behind her antennae?

The Abbot joined Rory, Angus and Esther at the rear of the ship, and he was smiling at the look of shock and horror on the faces of Angus and Esther. The Abbot was not afraid of Nessie, Rory thought! He stretched his arms out towards Angus and Esther and he directed them with a word, to go back to their baby, which they rushed to do, thinking that it may be the last time that they would get to hold him. The Abbot then turned towards Rory, and told him to signal Nessie away. Rory stood up on the highest board at the rear of the ship with the Abbot behind him, blocking him from the view of the crew and the passengers.

Nessie saw him, and she started to speed up towards the ship. Rory was sure that she was smiling, as he saw her razor-sharp teeth catch the sunlight and reflect towards him. A cry of fear and panic went up behind him. 'Everyone else thinks that Nessie is going to attack the ship,' he thought. Rory nodded his head towards her, and he signalled with his right hand for her to go away. With an obvious look of disappointment and sadness, she stopped her acceleration and she turned and swam back towards Fingal's Cave.

With one last sad look at Rory, she let out a squeal from her antennae and disappeared through the shimmering entrance.

Abbot Ian gave Rory a pat on the back and a conspiratorial wink, as they walked back to join Captain Roddy, Angus, Esther, Lee Chan and baby Eoin on the upper deck.

He whispered to Rory, saying, "Leave the talking to me."

The Abbot explained to the entire crew and the passengers that he had prayed for their salvation and that the monster had turned and left, just as it had previously when Saint Columba had ordered it away in Loch Ness. Rory was very brave, and he stood ready to fight it off with his sword in case the Abbot had been unable to command it away. Captain Roddy was not convinced, and he gave Rory a quizzical look. He remembered Rory signalling the giant Scottish Eagle away! There was something strange about this giant of a boy, who could command these powerful creatures and pull swords from stone floors!

The crew and all the passengers, except for Rory and Abbot Ian were badly shaken by their close encounter with Nessie; so much so that Captain Roddy went to his cabin and returned with three bottles of his special reserve whisky. He passed two bottles to the crew and kept one for himself and the passengers. The whisky moved quickly from hand to hand with even Lee Chan taking a generous nip, to fortify herself and it was quickly finished. As each took a drink, they gestured a toast raising the bottle, and giving a word of thanks to Nessie, for not destroying them.

Abbot Ian took the empty bottles and put a note in each one, and addressed them to Nessie and sealed all three bottles with a cork and wax. He then cast them overboard with a prayer of thanks, in front of the crew, which finished the process of calming them all down. Sailors were very superstitious, and Abbot Ian knew this.

From that day on, the story would be told of how the Abbot saved the ship from the monster, and that all religious disciples would have free travel on every ship in the world. They would be regarded as a good omen by all sailors and they were actively sought, and encouraged as free passengers.

Unknown to the Abbot he had also started the practice of a message in a bottle!

The Stag completed the short crossing from Staffa to the Abbey on Iona. Abbot Ian disembarked between all the crew who lined up either side of him, with their heads bowed. Rory followed him off the ship for a quick private word. The Abbot pointed out the large stone Abbey, to Rory which was a short distance away from the pier. He reminded Rory of his promise to Saint Columba, to return here to speak to him.

Rory knew that he would have to be in possession of the Hagpipe to do that, as he would have to go back in time. But his eight years prophesied without it, were drawing to an end with his sixteenth birthday fast approaching. He promised Abbot Ian that he would return as soon as circumstances permitted which he smiled at.

He was like Abbot MacCallum from Urquhart Castle and he seemed to know a great deal about Rory and the events that they both were being very secretive about. Rory boarded the Stag, deep in thought.

What was going to happen next and did they know?

CHAPTER 12

Homecoming

The Stag continued its journey, passing between the island of Iona and the large island of Mull and to the left between it and Lorne, into the Firth of Lorne, towards the Island of Lismore in the middle of the channel. Their ship passed the busy Island-hopping port of Oban on the left, as it was steered right past Lismore, where the Firth of Lorne joined the right-hand channel of the Sound of Mull, and left into Loch Linnhe. It was then a straight sail up Loch Linnhe past Ballachulish and Corran, and into the joining Loch of Aber.

A short sail later, Loch Aber was joining Loch Eil (IALL) where the gateway to the Highlands, Fort William, was situated shadowed by the highest mountain in Scotland Ben Nevis, which overlooked the twin Lochs. They were now officially in God's country, and on a sunny summer's day like today, it was the most beautiful place in the world.

The stone fort was situated on the loch side, overlooking both lochs, where they met, controlling the water, and protecting the town of Fort William. It had a long central main street, full of taverns and bars, on either side of a large central market.

It was also the end of the West Highland Way for the weary foot traveller who had completed it.[33]

The Stag docked at the central pier and Captain Roddy reported to the harbourmaster, paying and authorising the berthing of his ship.

The crew were given a very welcomed shore leave, to recover from the shock of seeing Nessie and were given the next day off. A few tales of their encounter with the monster would soon be circulating in every bar and retold and embellished with the encouragement of the story-teller, receiving a small refreshment (Whisky) with every new narration. It was just as well that they were not travelling the next day, and were able to recover.

Captain Roddy took his extended family and Rory to the nearby Guisachan Guest House, on the hillside overlooking the lochs, where he had resided before. It was more suited to accommodate the women and baby Eoin, and it was a vast improvement compared with the spit and sawdust tavern accommodation in the town, where the sailors were glad to stay sleeping where they fell. Roddy was warmly welcomed by the Landladies Betty and her younger sister Edith, who fussed over baby Eoin.

---

33 The West Highland Way (Scottish Gaelic: Slighe Na Gàidhealtachd an Iar) is officially the longest distance footpath in Scotland. It is 154.5 km (96.0 miles) long, and runs from Milngavie north of Glasgow to Fort William in the Scottish Highlands, with an element of hill walking in the route. It is not a stroll for the faint hearted and is most commonly walked by the well prepared for charity fundraising events.

Grandpa Roddy was congratulated, and Lee Chan and Esther were very happy at the home from home accommodation, and they felt very comfortable and welcome. Following a meal, Captain Roddy took Rory and Angus for a tour of the local hostelries, leaving the women to look after the baby. He had to go just to check up on his crew, you understand!

Everyone enjoyed their long lie on their soft feather mattresses and all were awakened at seven thirty, by bright sunshine streaming in at the windows and the alarm squeal of baby Eoin, wanting his breakfast. This did not help Rory's thumping head who just wanted to bury it below the pillows.

He had been forced to consume large amounts of beer and whisky after being pointed out as the man who had faced down the sea monster. He had lost count of the number of times he had to recall the tale and had a sore throat and a husky voice, as a result. He was keen on every telling making sure that the credit for Nessie leaving went to Abbot Ian Campbell, who fortunately for Rory, was not there to give his version of the story.

Rory got dressed in his summer kilt and shirt and checked that his sword and his cloth bag of possessions were safe below his bed, and then joined the rest of his companions for a full Scottish breakfast at a table in the communal dining room, next to the kitchen. The first person he saw was Captain Roddy, who, for a change, looked as rough as Rory felt.

This was mainly because he was the Captain of the ship that had faced the monster. He had been "encouraged" (by drinking whisky) by the other Captains, and the sailors, to narrate the "true" story of the encounter. Every pub and tavern got a different "true" story (more exaggerated with each telling), which seemed to be the sailor's way! Angus was no different health-wise than Rory and Roddy. Unfortunately, he received a very cold shoulder and icy looks from Esther, whose Mum was giving Roddy the same treatment. Angus was discovering that married life was not what had he expected and this made him feel a lot worse.

Partly restored by the massive fry up of bacon, eggs, haggis, black pudding, sausage and tattie scones, the men escaped the women, to arrange transport for Rory, Angus, Esther and the baby to Urquhart Castle, from the stables in the town. The market was on in the main street, and they passed stalls and carts full of goods for sale. Rory saw a stall selling early summer vegetables, with a pile of small carrots with long green stems. A strange feeling came over him, and he bought a good handful of them, tucking them into his kilt belt.

The next stall was selling jewellery, and had an impressive display of fresh water pearl necklaces. Rory thought of his Mum, who he would soon see again, and he knew that she would love one of these beautiful strings.

Rory still had plenty of money left and he began haggling over a price for a necklace. The vendor reduced his price slightly, and to seal the deal, threw in a silver ring with a Celtic word design around it, to confirm the purchase. Heather would love that Rory thought and he bought both.

They carried on to the stables which had a large paddock at its rear. Angus and Roddy went to look for a suitable two-seated carriage or cart, with soft springs and upholstery, to keep baby Eoin comfortable, on the trip to Urquhart Castle.

Rory went out the back to look at the horses, to see if he could find a suitable ride. He didn't have to look long, as he heard a neigh and the largest black stallion he had ever seen, came running up to him. It was Jet, his childhood horse, now fully grown and in his prime. Rory didn't know who was most pleased. He, at seeing Jet, or the other way round, as his horse nuzzled at his clothing, looking for carrots. Rory remembered the carrots in his belt, and he pulled them out. Jet snorted with pleasure, and pranced about in joy, at his reunion with Rory, who had remembered to bring him carrots.

'Is this what made me buy the carrots,' Rory thought, stunned at the coincidence that had just taken place, as he bought Jet, and a saddle, so that they both could return home to Urquhart Castle.

Roddy and Angus were equally successful getting a cart and two horses, on hire to Urquhart Castle, where the owner of the stables had an arrangement with Murdo Hands, for transport between the two places. The fact that they exchanged funny handshakes had "nothing" to do with it!

Rory saddled Jet, and accompanied by Roddy and Angus on the cart, returned to the Guisachan to uplift his possessions, Esther and baby Eoin. Rory put his sword and sheath over his back, putting the rest of his possessions in the cart. Angus collected all his possessions, and essential baby supplies, storing them in the cart, and he confirmed that the route to Urquhart Castle would take about a leisurely four hours, to reach.

It was then time for a sad farewell from Granny Lee and Grandpa Roddy as they waved baby Eoin away, along with Esther, Angus and Rory. This sad farewell was compensated by the fact that they would soon see the baby again in two weeks' time, when they visited Urquhart Castle for Rory's initiation.

Rory led the way, as they travelled out of Fort William. Ben Nevis loomed over them, next to its smaller sister mountain of Aonach Mor on their right, as they travelled along Glen Spean. They carried on to Spean Bridge, following the right side of Loch Lochy to Laggan.

The scenery was indescribably beautiful as they went on along the right side of Loch Oich to Fort Augustus, along the Great Glen and onto the left side of the start of Loch Ness. Rory felt sure that he was being watched, and he told Angus that he was riding ahead to check the route. He spurred Jet on who was desperate for a run, along the side of Loch Ness, as the length of the bottom section opened in front of him.

Rory was right; there in front of him looking straight at him from the middle of Loch Ness was Nessie. Just then a large rabbit was startled from the bracken on Rory's approach, and it ran from his left under Jet's hoofs. It was killed immediately, and it was probably the first road kill. Rory thought that this was lucky, and he recovered the rabbit. He told Jet to stay and he shook his head and his mane as if he understood, as Rory walked down to the banks of Loch Ness.

Nessie swam right up to Rory her massive long flexible neck bending towards him, as he threw the rabbit up in the air towards her. Just like the rat years before. she caught it easily in her mouth and swallowed it down. She bent her head down lower for Rory, who rubbed and tickled her behind her antennae as she let out high pitched squeals of pleasure.

Rory promised her that he would see her again soon, and she seemed to understand, as she turned and slowly submerged into the loch. She took one last look at Rory, with her intelligent grey /blue eyes in her otter-like head, atop her flexible long graceful neck, as it too slipped below the water.

A cart came around the bend in the road and Angus called out to Rory, and asked if he was all right as he had heard a strange squeal. Rory lied and said that he had seen some young foxes playing who were squealing, when he was answering a call of nature. Angus stopped the cart and said that he had to reply as well, and he jumped down.

A short time later they turned a right-hand bend, revealing the full length of Loch Ness and Urquhart Castle, standing proud in the sunlight, jutting into the Loch like a finger, testing the temperature.

The Abbot of Urquhart Malcolm MacCallum, had received a pigeon message from Iona Abbey that Rory was on his way home, along with Angus, his wife and baby Eoin and he had alerted his Mum and his friends. A watchman was placed at the top of the gatehouse, to look out for their passage along the Loch Road, and report to them and to a very excitable Heather, of their imminent arrival.

Rory was a striking figure as he arrived on his huge Jet-black stallion, in front of Angus and his family's cart. He was now six feet four, with a muscular frame, and a square-jawed tanned, handsome face which was framed by his shoulder-length red hair, blowing in the summer breeze. Strapped to his back on top of his short sleeved white shirt, showing off his bulging arm muscles was his Nessie/Haggis Sword. The ivory handle was reflecting the sun behind his head, giving the appearance of a halo around it!

Rory rode over the castle drawbridge between the twin towers of the gatehouse, to be met by all his friends and his acquaintances, with his mother at the head of the congregating group, with his now not so little brother Johnny, who had stretched, becoming taller than Heather who was standing next to her.

Rory's heart leapt, and it began to beat fast at the sight of her. He had forgotten how beautiful she was, as she stood in a light summer dress, showing off her now slim womanly figure, with her long dark hair blowing in the breeze.

He was experiencing some very strange feelings, and he had to be very careful, as he swung his kilted leg over the saddle, as he jumped to the ground. He had no sooner landed when Heather had launched herself into his arms, with hers around his neck, planting her lips on his. Rory could not help himself as he responded, kissing her back, much to the delight of his Mother.

She had become very close to Heather, who was like a daughter to her, and the surrounding crowd let out a cheer. The noise made Heather realise that she was being held up, off the ground, in Rory's arms and she went bright red in the face in embarrassment, as she was gently lowered onto her own feet.

Rory's Mum was next, lifted off the ground and into his arms. He was very careful with her, as he could feel her bones through her clothing and it was obvious to him that she had lost a lot of weight. He saw Granny Grant standing, waiting to welcome him, along with all his friends, and he made a mental note to speak to her about his Mum.

Angus and Esther with baby Eoin, waited patiently as the prodigal son was warmly welcomed, giving Esther the chance to think that her sister Jacqui had no chance of snaring Rory now, following that welcome by Heather, and Rory's response. They were approached by Rory's Mum Mary, who fussed over baby Eoin, and welcomed them to reside with her in her quarters in the Grant Tower, due to their new status, as heirs to the title of Lord and Lady of Skye.

The Constable, John Gregg stood nearby, and he had been in discussion with Abbot MacCallum, about Rory's sword, in relation to the ban on all weapons, within the castle grounds.

It was decided to make an exception in Rory's case, as the stories about this sword had already reached Urquhart Castle, and he didn't fancy having to guard it twenty-four hours a day. It was already causing quite a stir, as a queue was forming next to Rory, of warriors wanting to see it.

Wee Charlie Campbell had managed to squeeze past them, to greet Rory and he was being shown the sword at present, and was being laughed at for not being able to hold it. He was fully qualified as a saddler now, and he paid a great deal of attention to the dimensions of the sword, for a surprise for Rory's birthday.

Charlie was slightly older, and a lot shorter than Rory, and he had already had his manhood initiation, and he looked forward to watching Rory get his, knowing the surprise that awaited him. The crowd gathering around Rory, had the potential for getting out of order, as some of the more boisterous warriors became frustrated at not being able to hold the sword.

Before the Constable had to take any action, the shawled, hunched figure of Granny Grant walked to the front of the bickering warriors. She easily picked up Rory's sword by its Haggis/Nessie grip, and walked off with it towards her home. The warriors all stood with their mouths open, at the sight of this small old woman, lifting the long, heavy sword.

The ones who could not hold it, began to be teased by their pals, and they began to make excuses of trickery, saying that the grip could have been greased and that Granny was using her plaid to hold it. Good humour was restored, at the sight of the giant Rory, running off after Granny Grant, to get his sword back, like a wee boy after his favourite toy.

Rory saw a stable boy guide Jet or more to the point, Jet guided the stable boy to the stables, as he was keen to return home as well, as he caught up with Granny Grant.

Her intervention had calmed things down and the castle was returning to normality. Rory sat with her at the fire outside her cabin, and he asked how she could lift the sword, as she returned it to him to be sheathed.

She only replied that they were old friends, which really confused Rory.

'How could that be, another mystery?'

He tried his luck and he asked Granny about his Mum's health. She was pleased with this change in conversation, as she did not want to be pressed to speak about her knowledge of the sword. A look of concern came over her face as she said that his mum had been very ill and that she was treating her to the best of her ability, but even she would not be able to cure her.

This really worried Rory, at the honesty of Granny Grant, and with a tear in his eye, he asked if she was going to die. She said that everyone dies, but unless a miracle happened that she wouldn't see another summer. Rory was devastated, as Granny gave him a cuddle and a plate of her special Haggis, which made him feel slightly better. It was a more subdued Rory, who returned to his old room above the foundry, that had had a new, much larger bed put in it, along with his possessions from the cart.

He was not much in the mood to catch up with Pally Ally and the other blacksmiths, and he had an early night.

CHAPTER 13

Initiation

Rory remained in a very black mood and he felt guilty at having left his Mum to go to Dunscaith Castle, when she needed him. Hamish Cooper had told him that his Stepdad John Grant had moved out of Grant Tower to quarters in the main castle, showing no interest in his sick wife. Everyone appeared to know of his Mum's illness and all were very sympathetic to Rory's feelings.

He visited his Mum in Grant Tower who sat eating some of Granny Grant's extra special Haggis which Granny had said she was giving her once a week to bolster her strength. Granny had told Rory that she had received the shavings from the left tusk of the first Haggis which Abbot MacCallum carved to make his sword grip. This was very special, and its magical properties when ground and put in the Haggis, would increase his Mum's strength against the bone illness that she had. Granny had a very small supply of it and she rationed it, giving it to her once a week, to keep his Mum alive.

His Mum was in a lot of pain and Esther had noticed that she was quite ill. She told Rory that she knew an ancient Chinese medicine that would take away the pain that his Mum felt, but she too couldn't cure her of the illness. Rory was practically in tears at this offer from Esther, and he agreed to her help. She showed him a small box containing long thin needles which she said when placed in certain places of the body would stop her from feeling any pain.[34]

Rory was glad for any help as he looked at the sallow skin on his Mum's smiling face, as she looked at him. As Rory watched his Mum eat the special Haggis, her skin regained its normal colour, which pleased him. It was agreed with Esther for her to begin her treatment when she had noticed the colour begin to change, as she would need it most at that time. He gave his Mum her present of the pearl necklace, that he had bought in Fort William, which she put on immediately with a huge smile and a kiss of thanks.

Rory vowed to rescue his Dad at his first opportunity, so that he could see that smile again before she died!

His father Ruaidri had spent the last thirteen years in enslavement to the Vikings, under King Haakon, manacled hand and foot and put to work rowing a longboat, with other slaves, all chained together.

Only the thought of his wife Mary and his son Rory gave him the willpower to keep going, and the fact that as he was part of the fleet of one hundred and twenty ships leaving Bergen. The slaves were given more food to strengthen them for their ordeal ahead. King Haakon was determined to reinforce his control on the Hebrides

---

34 Acupuncture (from the Latin, acus (needle) and punctura (to puncture) is a form of alternative medicine and a key component of traditional Chinese medicine involving thin needles inserted into the body at acupuncture points and is commonly used for pain relief. Excerpt from Wikipedia.

Islands, following a raid by King Alexander III of Scotland to these Islands in 1262. Ruaidri had overheard that he was going to be part of the main fleet of about one hundred longboats detailed for a major attack on the Scottish Army in the affluent west coast of Scotland near Largs.

Ruaidri was elated to return to Scotland, and he was hopeful that he might get a chance to escape and to find a way home!

Rory awoke on the morning of his sixteenth birthday on the twenty fourth of June, the day that he knew that he was preordained to recover the Hagpipe and to save his Dad. He didn't feel any different, and outside it looked like any other slightly cloudy summer's day. There was a knock on the door and he opened it to see the beaming face of Wee Charlie Campbell, looking back at him, wishing him a happy birthday.

Charlie held out a new hard leather long sword sheath, lined and reinforced with lead with double shoulder straps. Rory looked at it surprised at the craftsmanship involved in its construction with an embossed sunken impression along its length, depicting Nessie swimming along Loch Ness. He warmly thanked the beaming Charlie who was very happy at Rory's reaction, as he swiftly removed his sword from its battered sheath and slid it into the new one with a hiss. It fitted perfectly.

'Charlie has a very precise eye for detail,' Rory thought.

Rory tied the new harness onto his back where it shaped itself comfortably to his body like a hand in a glove without needing any adjustment. He reached back with both hands. The sword flew out of the sheath into his hands again with a hiss similar to the noise made by Esther's sword when she had removed it from its sheath.

Charlie was ecstatic with delight at this display from his dear friend who was the happiest he had seen him in two weeks. Rory returned the sword again with the hiss of a snake and dug deep into his sporran. He removed the old worn leather thong that he had retained from the Hagpipe and asked Charlie if he could make him a new one. Charlie looked at it and said that it would be no problem and he would treat the end that attaches with a sap like glue so that it wouldn't fall off again.

'How did Charlie know that!' Rory thought.

The blacksmiths Pally Ally, Jimmy Black and Gordon Grant were waiting for him in the foundry along with Abbott Malcolm MacCallum and Hamish Cooper accompanied with his wife Moira and now daughter Heather as he walked down the stairs in his full highland one-piece kilt with his sword on his back and sturdy boots on his feet. Rory was a very imposing figure and he looked ready for business and heaven help anyone who stood in his way.

Moira had cooked a birthday breakfast for everyone who waited patiently to give him presents. The biggest was a warm birthday kiss from Heather who had to be practically prized off Rory.

Abbot Malcolm gave Rory a present of a new Sgian Dubh (Skein Dubh), which he said all the blacksmiths had a part in making. It was razor sharp with a Haggis engraved on each side of the blade, topped with a small oval of Ivory from the same large left first haggis tusk comprising the grip on his sword. As Rory took it he felt his sword on his back shiver in acknowledgement of all its parts being reunited and whole again. Abbot MacCallum had informed Rory that no weapon could pass through the portal unless it was part of the first Haggis, so he was now well equipped with two as he put his new Sgian Dubh in his right sock in its scabbard.

After breakfast Rory stopped for a short visit to Granny Grant to uplift the weekly dose of extra special Haggis for his Mum. The supply of the magical ground tusk powder was becoming very low and she didn't know how much more she could ration it. She said that she was putting a full measure of it in today's Haggis to give his Mum a boost for his birthday.

Rory took it to his Mum who was still in bed sleeping, being watched by a worried looking Esther. Rory coaxed his Mum awake, who rallied at seeing him and he spoon fed her the Haggis washing it down with a cup of tea. The Haggis worked, and she became alert and regained a healthy glow and wished him a happy birthday. She said that she had not got him a present and Rory said that she was present enough and gave her a big hug.

His Mum was now strong enough to join Angus, Esther, Rory and baby Eoin to walk to the water gate. The Stag had been spotted sailing down Loch Ness. It was filled-up with a delegation from all the Highland Clans who Rory had met at Angus and Esther's wedding, who as promised, were coming for Rory's Initiation. It was highly unusual for so many Clans to be in such close proximity to one another, unless they were fighting but they all seemed to be in high spirits and being unusually friendly with one another, like brothers.

Captain Roddy berthed the Stag, facing outward onto Loch Ness at the long pier, securing it with a heavy rope as he and Lee Chan followed the thirsty Clan Warriors into Urquhart Castle, where they surrendered their weapons without any dispute with the Constable.

Both rushed to their grandson, ignoring Angus and Esther, gushing and cooing at him, saying, "What a big boy you are and how you've grown," much to their amusement.

Evening came, with the main event of Rory's initiation and the chapel was full of the visitors who had been tested on entering to prove their eligibility to attend. Every trade and profession was represented from Stone Masons to Coopers. with Rory's friends sitting together in the front row, facing the chequered floor. As with Ally, when he was initiated, Rory went to the refectory where his sword, sporran and Sgian Dubh were removed, leaving him in his full plaid Mac Sween tartan highland kilt. Rory immediately recognised the two wardens clothed in full length brown robes with hoods over their heads, who were preparing him for his initiation.

They were Hamish Cooper and Jimmy Black. He was glad to see their friendly faces, and to hear their assurance that they would be by his side throughout his trials, and that he had nothing to fear. Both walked him over to the door of the temple, carrying his possessions where Rory saw the huge frame who he recognised now as the Constable, standing holding his long sword vertically to the ground. He was wearing a similar long brown robe with the hood over his head, but he was the only person in the castle bigger than Rory. A black hood was placed over Rory's head, preventing him from seeing anything, and Rory recognised the Constable's voice who questioned Hamish, who was holding his left arm. Hamish whispered an answer that he could not make out.

Rory then heard three loud knocks on the door, which opened to a hushed silence from within. He was led into the temple and felt as if he had walked for miles, as he was led around it three times and then helped to kneel in front of a large stone object, which he recognised as the altar. Rory then recognised a very familiar voice speaking to him. It was Abbot MacCallum, who asked Rory to repeat his words in a long-winded speech, basically making him promise to keep what he was about to be told secret.

At the end of the oath he was asked if he wanted anything and Rory replied, "To see".

Rory felt the hood being removed, as he heard deafening loud clapping like thunder, made by those watching the ceremony and as he blinked his eyes, he saw that he was bathed in a beam of rainbow colours of light streaming in from the left stained-glass window depicting Saint Columba. The Abbot stood in front of him wearing a similar purple robe, just like the one in the stained-glass image of Saint Columba. He was standing on the opposite side of the Altar, which contained the book of Saint Columba, his sword, Sgian Dubh and sporran.

Rory was told that he would now be put in possession of the identifying handshake and password of a

Warrior of H.A.G.I and that he would travel to the four points of the temple where he would be told the meaning of the letters.

Abbot MacCallum walked around to Rory and took hold of his right hand pressing the first three fingers of his hand into the palm of his hand with his thumb on the top, asking Rory to do the same, whilst covering the top of his hand with his left. He explained that this was the identifying hand shake of all initiates, but it was not complete without whispering the word which had to be shared by alternative letters between those shaking. He explained the letters were H.A.G.I. and he made Rory repeat the process until he knew it.

This is what the funny handshake was, Rory realised, and he knew it now!

He was led by Hamish to the first point in the north of the temple, where he stood with him below the letter I. Jimmy Black then explained the meaning of the letter which stood for Invisible. He then turned Rory to face the stained-glass windows in the east of the temple, where from this angle, the last of the evening sunshine was beaming upwards into the top left-hand corner of the left window of Saint Columba. Rory was told to focus on the top left corner, and as he watched, the light was diffracted by the red glow of the sun, showing the outline of a Great Scottish Eagle. It was the perfect image of Ben the Eagle, his friend!

Rory was then led to the south point of the temple where he was placed under the letter A. Hamish narrated a short lecture on the Animal of the Loch, which was the

Ali of Man, and was not an animal to be feared[35]. He was turned to the East again where the stained-glass image of Nessie was pointed out.

He was then walked to the East and placed again in front of the Altar, and below the letter G. Jimmy Black then gave a lecture on the Great One who controlled all three mythical animals, which was why the handshake used three fingers. The great one was pointed out in the left stained-glass window. It wasn't Saint Columba as Rory expected.

The small boy standing next to him! It was Rory!

He was reeling at this revelation, as his sporran; Sgian Dubh and sword were returned to him and put back on. He was informed that he was going to impersonate the Great One, and that he would need his possessions back and he was led to the West end of the temple. He was placed below the letter H, and was not surprised when he was informed by Hamish that it stood for Haggis.

He was surprised when he was told that to complete his initiation he was to kill it!

Hag had been looking for Rory since he had left the Nessie cave and the rowing boat had disappeared.[36].

She had left through the orange/yellow light of the portal, to the main cave below the castle, to see the rowing boat appear on the beach. She rushed over to it, to welcome Rory, but he was not there.

---

35 Anagram for animal, Ali Man.
36 Refer to Book 1: The Secrets of Urquhart Castle.

In the bottom of the boat, without the thong, was the Hagpipe!

Hag carefully lifted it in her snout, and walked to the cave of the Haggis Graveyard giving a short squeal, activating the lava coloured curtain and she walked in. The cave was empty. There was no pile of tusks, just an empty stone circle on the ground like a nest. Hag placed the Hagpipe in the nest, where she had been born, and left the cave to continue her long search through time for Rory.

Four initiated castle warriors had been up at the break of dawn to prepare for Rory's initiation. They went to the temple, armed with nets and a large metal cage, and went down the secret stairwell to the large cave below Urquhart Castle. They crossed Loch Ness to the far shore in the large rowing boat where there was a more plentiful supply of wild Haggis. They did not have to climb far up the mountain, when they saw the largest Haggis that they had ever seen. It was a mature female about the size of a large sheep, with large leathery wings on its back, with huge pointed tusks either side of a mouth with razor sharp teeth. It was standing on its uneven legs over a small deer, that it was enjoying for its breakfast.

Their legs shook as they sneaked up behind it and threw the net over the Haggis. It did not struggle, and it let them easily push it into the metal cage which they bolted shut. 'It must be old and dim witted,' they thought. It could have easily killed them if it wanted to, being so large. They lifted the cage with long poles pushed through the bars either side at the top as the docile Haggis looked at them with its squinty eyes. The brave warriors returned to the castle for an early drink pleased at their great hunting skills.

Rory still faced the west wall of the temple with his head now recovered by the hood unable to see. He heard the scraping noise of the secret door in the east wall opening, and the metal cage being dragged in. He heard gasps behind him, as those watching the initiation saw the size of the Haggis in the cage. He heard a couple of voices congratulating the warriors who had captured this beast.

The brave warriors were expecting these congratulations to transform into free whisky at the end of the night. They sat in the north east corner near to the cage, with their swords below the pew, in case Rory failed to kill the Haggis. They were full of confidence that they would not be needed. They knew that the cage was strong and that the Haggis was stupid and docile. What could possibly go wrong?

Rory's hood was removed, and he was instructed to turn and to approach the Haggis from the rear and kill it with a sword blow to the base of the neck in warrior fashion. The light was failing in the temple as he cautiously approached the cage. He saw the massive Haggis sniff the air and turn its head to the left, so that it could see behind it with the right eye on the top of its head. It saw the approaching warrior with the drawn sword, and let out a massive squeal, and reared in the cage, bending and breaking the bars as if they were twigs.

The cage collapsed into pieces as the Haggis turned and reared again as the brave warriors who were meant to intervene jumped from their seats and ran from the temple to escape. Panic ensued, no one else had weapons and warriors began climbing over the pews to get as far from this ferocious beast as possible.

The squeal sounded very familiar to Rory, as did the smiling face not the snarling one everyone else saw, looking at him. The Haggis was not angry showing it teeth, it was Hag his pet, and she was smiling and very, very happy to see him.

They both ran at one another and they were soon rolling about on the chequered floor like a small boy playing with his puppy. Rory tickled Hag behind her ears, as she squealed in delight and rolled on her back for him to tickle her belly. The temple was in an uproar. No one could believe what they were seeing.

Well maybe one, as Abbot Malcolm MacCallum stood over the book of Saint Columba which was open at a picture of this very scene!

CHAPTER 14

Rescue

The reunion was over, and Hag sat at Rory's left side lovingly looking up at him with her squinty eyes. Very few were brave enough to approach Rory, but Wee Charlie Campbell cautiously walked up to him holding a small thin leather skin parcel.

"You will need this Great One," he said with a wry smile.

Rory took the parcel from him with a nod and they exchanged the new handshake he had learned from him. Rory then turned with Hag towards the still open concealed door to the spiral staircase leading to the cave below. He bid farewell to all and he left the temple to follow Hag down the gloomy lit spiral stairs, until the door closed behind him and plunged him into darkness.

The meeting then closed, as everyone retired to the refectory for a well needed drink and to reflect on what had just happened!

From Rory's point of view, he had been separated from Hag for eight years. From the point of view of Hag, only a year had passed as she, Nessie and Ben the Eagle searched for him not only by location but in different time periods. They had travelled through the various portals located in the stone circles and natural caves, connected to the lay line network. This caused many sightings of them, creating the myths of today some of which are well documented like the doctor's photograph of Nessie in Loch Ness. If he had only raised his camera a few inches towards the sky he would have really caused a stir with a photograph of a fully-grown female Haggis flying, tilted to her right-hand side, so that she could scan the ground with her uneven eyes. That really would have taken some explaining!

Rory lit a torch inside the dark stairwell and walked down the right-hand spiralling stone steps, following Hag who ran down them easily, with her two long left legs and shorter right ones. They entered the sandy beach of the large cave, with the last of the night's sunshine reflecting on the still water, from the exit to Loch Ness.

He put the torch out and left it at the stairs and followed a very excitable Hag towards the cave of the Haggis Graveyard. Rory stood at the entrance knowing that if he stepped inside he would find an empty cave. Hag looked at him and she let out a high-pitched squeal. The entrance illuminated in dark lava red and shimmered and together they both stepped inside. The cave was reasonably lit by the reflective roof crystals and Rory could see that the cave was empty. The huge mound of Haggis Tusks of the graveyard were missing and he was sure that Hag must have made a mistake by activating the portal.

She was very excited and she danced about around his ankles wanting him to follow her. Rory followed her to the centre of the cave where the graveyard had been, and he looked down at the stone circular nest where he had first found Hag as an egg. In its centre was the Hagpipe!

He had found it! He could save his father now, and he was quite overcome with emotion, letting a tear run down his face. His wait was over!

He reached down and lifted the Hagpipe with his right hand. A euphoric surge of power ran through his body, as all his senses and his abilities were multiplied by his age. His skin went as hard as iron, and he felt indestructible. Anything was possible for him now!

Rory could hear a sweet girl's voice in his head. He concentrated on listening to it and it said, "Dad."

He looked down to see Hag sitting at his feet, looking up at him smiling. 'I can hear Hag now,' Rory thought. 'Can she hear me?'

The voice came again, "Of course I can," as Hag reared up, putting her front legs on his. He tickled her behind her ears as he heard her laughing in his head. It took a lot of getting used to, but he would never be lonely again unless he put the Hagpipe down, but first he had to rescue his Dad.

He took the package that Charlie had given him from his sporran, and he unwrapped it, revealing a new thong for the Hagpipe. The loop which pushed over the narrow end of it was covered in a very sticky clear substance. Rory fitted it onto the Hagpipe which stuck fast, and it began to dry quickly as the Hagpipe went warm in his hand.

Rory put the Hagpipe attached to the new thong, on over his head, determined that he would never be parted from it again. At that time the area in front of him next to the nest began to shimmer in a white light. Rory and Hag stepped back away from it, as the intensity of the light increased until it was so blindingly white, that he had to cover his eyes. The light went out and he uncovered his eyes to see the mound of tusks of the Haggis Graveyard in front of him!

Everything was back to normal. All he had to do now was to rescue his Dad and he had a plan to do that, but first he would need a ship. Rory was sure that Captain Roddy wouldn't mind him borrowing the Stag. Well not much, if he brought it back in one piece! The other thing that he would need would be Nessie's help.

Hag still read his mind as she squealed, opening the portal back to the main cave. They stepped through and Rory raised the Hagpipe to his mouth and gave it a blow. Almost immediately a long graceful neck emerged from the water in front of him and Nessie looked at him.

Rory heard another older woman's voice in his head, scolding him saying, "You only had to ask, there's no need to command me."

For the second time Rory was taken aback, Nessie could talk to him as well. He heard Hag laughing in his head, as he mentally apologised and he heard Nessie reply, by accepting the apology, and asking what she could do for him. Rory understood now and if they could speak to one another then it followed that he and they could talk to Ben as well.

He heard both voices agreeing with him, and if he concentrated he could hear the conversation that they were having between them and join in. This was going to be a lot of fun, and a lot easier than he had imagined, as he mentally talked his plan out with Hag and Nessie. The rowing boat was still tethered to the post on the beach, and Rory untied it. He moved it, facing outwards towards the cave exit, and he and Hag jumped in. He tied the long securing rope in a large loop and threw it into the deep water.

Nessie put her head threw the noose below the water and pulled them out the cave and around to the pier where the Stag was berthed, facing out onto the loch. Rory tied up the rowing boat, as Hag flew up to the pier, as she was unable to climb the vertical steps. Rory checked that the Stag was unoccupied and that all of the crew were on shore leave. Most of them were in the refectory, enjoying some free hospitality, following his initiation.

No one saw Rory as he untied the ship from the pier and tied the anchor rope in a large loop and threw it over the front of the ship into the Loch. The rope floated briefly on top of the water as the head of Nessie's smiling face popped up through the middle of it. She easily towed the Stag out into the Loch and back towards the cave entrance.

Rory stood at the front of the ship and he raised the Hagpipe to his mouth with his right hand. He cleared his head and visualized the picture of the Battle of Largs that he had seen in the Book of Saint Columba in 1263 and Fingal's Cave. The Portal illuminated dark orange in front of him as Nessie towed the Stag through it and out of Fingal's Cave, back in time and into the middle of a major storm.[37]

---

37 The recorded historic account of the Battle of Largs is as follows: The Battle of Largs (2 October 1263) was an indecisive engagement between the kingdoms of Norway and Scotland near Largs, Scotland. The conflict formed part of the Norwegian expedition against Scotland in 1263, in which Hakon Hakonarson, the King of Norway attempted to reassert Norwegian sovereignty over the western seaboard of Scotland. Since the beginning of the twelfth century this region had lain within the Norwegian realm, ruled by magnates who recognised the overlordship of the Kings of Norway.

However, in the mid-thirteenth century, two Scottish kings, Alexander the second, and his son Alexander the third, attempted to incorporate the region into their own realm. Following failed attempts to purchase the islands from the Norwegian King, the Scots launched military operations. Hakon responded to the Scottish aggression by leading a massive fleet from Norway, which reached the Hebrides in the summer of 1263. By the end of September, Hakon's fleet occupied the Firth of Clyde, and when negotiations between the kingdoms broke down, he brought the bulk of his fleet to anchor off the Cumbraes.

On the night of the thirtieth of September, during a bout of particularly stormy weather, several Norwegian vessels were driven aground on the Ayrshire coast, near the present-day town of Largs.

On the second of October, while the Norwegians were salvaging their vessels, the main Scottish army arrived on the scene. Composed of infantry and cavalry, the Scottish force was commanded by Alexander of Dundonald, Steward of Scotland. The Norwegians were gathered in two groups: the larger main force on the beach and a small contingent atop a nearby mound. The advance of the Scots threatened to divide the Norwegian

Now this is what really Happened!

It was a very nasty storm with sweeping rain and high winds and still higher waves in the choppy open sea. Rory realised he might have been over confident about the ease of this rescue mission. The Stag was being battered about from side to side, and was in danger of subsiding, as the large waves hit it from all angles. He took hold of the Hagpipe, so that he would not lose it as he was thrown about the deck of the ship. The Hagpipe went

---

forces, so the contingent upon the mound ran to re-join their comrades on the beach below.

Seeing them running from the mound, the Norwegians on the beach believed that they were retreating, and had fled back towards their ships. Fierce fighting took place on the beach, and the Scots took up a position on the mound. formerly held by the Norwegians. Late in the day, after several hours of skirmishing, the Norwegians were able to recapture the mound.

The Scots withdrew from the scene and the Norwegians were able to board their ships. They returned the next morning to collect their dead. The weather had deteriorated, and Hakon's demoralised forces turned for home.

Hakon's campaign had failed to maintain Norwegian overlordship of the seaboard, and his native magnates, left to fend for themselves, were soon forced to submit to the Scots.

King Haakon Haakonsson then over-wintered at the Bishop's Palace in Kirkwall, Orkney, with plans to resume his campaign the next year. During his stay in Kirkwall, however, he fell ill and died in the early hours of the sixteenth of December 1263.

Three years after the battle, with the conclusion of the Treaty of Perth, Magnus Hakonarson the succeeding King of Norway ceded Scotland's western seaboard to Alexander the third, and thus the centuries-old territorial dispute between the consolidating kingdoms was at last settled. Excerpt from Wikipedia.

hot in his right hand, as his feet seemed to grow roots into the deck. The ship stabilized in the water as he felt power flow from him into the floorboards and along the rope around Nessie's neck.

Nessie was filled with the power of the Hagpipe and Rory heard her thank him in his head, as she took off at high, speed towing the Stag like a speedboat through the waves. Hag was receiving power, as she sat at his feet, oblivious to the storm around her, as if she was an unmoveable statue. The Stag tore past the Islands of Iona, Colonsay and Islay over the channel of the Sound of Jura, and into the deep waters of the North Channel.

They hit the strong northerly current of the North Atlantic Drift with the elements and effects of the storm having no effect on their progress, as the ship was whizzed left by Nessie into the Firth of Clyde. The mini Scotland of the large Island of Arran with its unique eco balance of botanic and mountainous zones with the biggest mountain 'Goat Fell,' filled the skyline.

They flew past it along the west coast towards Largs, as Nessie slowed her approach and stopped. Rory could see why with his now enhanced eyesight.

In front of him off the coastline at Portencross Castle which overlooks the approach to the channel between the twin Cumbrae Islands of Cumbrae and Little Cumbrae, was the imposing fleet of one hundred longboats, full of ferocious Vikings armed to the teeth with broadswords and fighting axes.

He saw the Scottish Army marching along the coastal road to Largs, which he estimated would be overwhelmed by this force. Rory knew that he would have to do something to balance the numbers for a fair fight and this storm would be a good excuse to cover the use of his abilities. But he needed a good pair of eyes in the sky to keep his Dad safe. He raised the Hagpipe to his mouth and blew it, thinking of Ben the Great Scottish Eagle.

Almost instantaneously Ben appeared above the Stag. He had heard the call like he did when he passed through the Portal at Callanish on Lewis. This may even be the same call Rory thought!

A deep male voice boomed in Rory's head asking," How can I help?"

Rory thanked Ben for coming and he was very pleased that Rory could 'talk' at last. He explained that he wanted Ben to identify the longboat that his father was on, and that he would direct Nessie to sink the others. Nessie was very happy at getting to play with the small boats, which she always wanted to do for just for a laugh. This agreed, Nessie slipped out of the anchor rope and submerged, leaving her head sticking up like a periscope.

Rory was concerned about the innocent crew of slaves in the longboats, and communicated this to Nessie and to Ben. Nessie suggested that Rory could balance like a surfer on her back between her neck and first hump, and jump on each ship as she approached them. He would have to fight all the Vikings on board, to release the slaves. To do this would take too much time, Rory thought. He would have to do this for a hundred ships, and they would be able to get organised and escape.

Ben said he could carry him on his neck to save his feet from getting wet, and drop him on the ships. Either way, he would have to fight the invading Viking Army on each longboat.

There must be an easier way?

The problem was that the slaves were chained in their seats. This was the solution he decided, and Rory asked Nessie to tip each longboat upside down, throwing all the Vikings off the longboat and into the sea, and then to right the ship again. The slaves rowing it would be safe, chained to their seats, albeit that they would get wet and have to hold their breath for a short time.

Ben quickly flew over the Armada, identifying the longboat that Rory's Dad was on, and he told Nessie, who got to work opening a path through the middle of the Armada. Rory had heard the conversation between Ben and Nessie as she submerged below the first targeted longboat, nudging it over with her humps and then pushing it upright again, by its mast, after turning it upside down in the sea.[38]

The sea was incredibly cold and the heavily armoured Vikings would sink like stones, unless they quickly disarmed and swam for the shore. The sight of a fully-grown

---

38 The water off the coast of the Island of Cumbrae is one of the deepest areas of sea in the world and today it is still the site of a marine training station with decompression chambers. It is also a channel for nuclear submarines heading to and from their not so secret base at Faslane. Nessie would have loved to play with these toys!

Loch Ness Monster swimming next to them was a great motivation to move very fast.

Rory heard Nessie laughing in his head at the fun that she was having, as Ben flew to the front of the Stag and asked Rory to jump in the air as high as he could. With the power of the Hagpipe multiplying his own abilities he could jump sixteen times higher than normal and he soared thirty feet into the air.

Ben flew under him, as he came back down, and Rory landed on the back of his neck behind his head. The Hagpipe warmly pulsed against his chest and flowed down his legs, filling Ben with its power to his great delight. He flew in a blur to each longboat, now divested of its Viking Army. A quick jump from Ben's neck saw Rory land lightly on board the first longboat where he thought of Hans the Sword. It jumped out of its sheath on his back, and into his hands. Rory cut though the retaining chains running from the front to the back of the longboat on each side, like butter.

The slaves were wet and cold, but otherwise they were unhurt by their spin in the sea. They had more difficulty coming to terms with seeing a massive Scottish Eagle hovering above them, and for the unlucky few who had their eyes open as the ship rotated, the sight of Nessie pushing it upright.

They were terrified at the sight of these massive monsters, as Rory shouted, "You're free!"

He jumped back into the air and to the eyes of the watching slaves he had flown onto the neck of the huge bird which unbelievably for them, obeyed his silent commands. Ben flew to the next longboat which had been washed clean of the Vikings, where the process was completed again and again, at breathtaking speed.

The slaves pulled the chains connecting them through the retaining ring on their foot manacles, and they stood up and stretched, amazed at the events and the manner of their freedom. They watched as their comrades on the adjoining longboats were freed and rowed over to join them. All the freed longboats were soon tied together in the middle of the channel and exchanged family members and countrymen, to travel home together.

Only one Viking longboat was left sitting alone in the middle of the channel. Nessie swam towards it, smiling as she went at the Vikings on board. The rest of the fleet had followed the leadership of their King, who had watched in horror, as he witnessed one by one as each longboat had rotated in the water before him. Even in the gloom of the storm, briefly illuminated with flashes of lightning, he had seen the huge sea monster attacking his longboats, and the massive bird which looked as if it had two heads, that hovered over the rotated ships. King Haakon fled for his life, for the first time feeling what fear felt like. He had heard stories which he had not believed until now of this monster of the deep, dismissing them to himself, as the ramblings of the drunk and demented, but they were all true. He was a broken man as he instructed his fleet to flee back to the safety of Kirkwall to reassess his plans.

The crew of the last lone longboat saw the razor-sharp shiny teeth of Nessie glowing, as a flash of lightning bounced off them as she swam towards them. They had watched the commotion around them as the fleet had rotated upside down, and upright again, in the sea, and they terrifyingly now knew why!

It was quite amazing how fast Vikings could swim as they dumped their weapons and their armour and ran to the opposite side of the longboat, away from Nessie, and dived into the sea. They swam for the coast and left the slave crew to their fate, thinking that this monster had despatched all in its wake, and that it could snack on them, while they escaped. Rory dropped softly from the sky onto the rear deck of the dry longboat from Ben's neck. The last super brave Viking and captain of the longboat watched open-mouthed, and had quickly reassessed things as he had stayed to defend it, and the plunder that he had taken. All thoughts of the reward that he would have received from his king were driven from his mind, as he too dived from his longboat and swam for the shore.

Rory took his time now, he paid attention to the emaciated group of slaves manacled hand and foot. He felt angry at the treatment of these men and was disappointed that all the Vikings had fled the longboat. He had an urge to punish them, as Hans the Sword again flew into his hands with a hiss, making him ready to fight. His anger rose like a red mist behind his eye balls. The sword intensified his urge for battle and Rory felt its craving for death and blood, which he had to consciously fight down.

He looked to the shore where a large number of bedraggled waterlogged Vikings were being easily subdued and either put to flight or captured by the inferior but dryer and fitter Scottish Army, who were dominating them.

The tide had turned, so to speak, and the Viking force was facing imminent defeat.

'The Scottish Army do not need any more help to finish them off,' Rory thought. The Vikings who had witnessed Nessie and Ben had no heart for a fight. How can you fight a monster?

But from this day on every new longboat that was built by the Vikings would have a monster's head at the front of their ships, to terrify their enemies!

With one blow to the retaining chains either side of the longboat, Rory struck them and they shattered. He walked along the ship, to help and free all the bewildered slaves and he froze like a statue as he reached the last row. In front of him was an older skinny version of himself, with greying red matted hair, wearing a very well-worn Mac Sween highland kilt!

It was his Dad!

He recognised Rory too. He could have been his double twenty years earlier. With a quick blow Rory shattered his remaining chains and helped the weak, frail man to his feet.

He said, "Dad" and he embraced Ruaidri warmly, in his arms, feeling his skeletal frame, as they both began to cry and hug one another; lost in the intensity of their feelings at being reunited after having been so long apart.

The rest of the slave crew were from various parts of the Islands and Highlands of Scotland, with some from Ireland and they watched this emotional reunion, thinking of their own loved ones. They became fully immersed in the moment, losing control of their own feelings, crying at the thought that they too would soon be experiencing the same joy with their own families.

None of the now free men were more caught up in this than John Hamilton from Ayrshire, who had been captured at the same time as Ruaidri, following a Viking Raid on Kerelaw Castle (Kerala), his family home in Stivenstoune, now known as Stevenston. He and Ruaidri had become close friends and allies, and both were Brothers of Haggai, and they had vowed to protect one another. But he had another person to care for, and to protect now as he looked at the hunched slim figure, that cowered at the front of the longboat, wrapped in a baggy brown monk's robe. She was Maura, the last survivor from the recent successful raid on a monastery and an adjacent Priory of the Knights of Saint Columba, on the nearby Island of little Cumbrae.

Maura had only survived due to her sex, as even the Vikings refused to kill a woman, especially a woman Monk. A very rare prize for King Haakon to go with the great treasure that they had recovered in the raid. The Vikings had looked for this fabled treasure since it was first brought to Scotland by the fleeing Templars from ACRE, and was moved from one religious' site to the next, to keep it hidden.

That was until Rory intervened with Nessie and Ben to rescue his Dad.

Rory informed the leader of the freemen, John Hamilton, that the longboat was now theirs to go home, totally unaware of the vast treasure in its hold. The survivors searched the well supplied boat for food and drink and warm clothing, as Ruaidri said an emotional farewell to his friend John, who he would never see again. He knew that he would be travelling forward in time to be reunited with his wife Mary, and by then his friend would have been dead for a very long time.

They parted with a secret handshake and a silent look of understanding, regarding the treasure that Ruaidri might someday tell Rory about. Ruaidri was helped into the Stag, by Rory, as John Hamilton joined the rest of the freed slaves congregating in the middle of the channel, in their longboats, exchanging countrymen and friends. John Hamilton had literally handpicked his Brothers of H.A.G.I, who he could trust to return with him and take the treasure to Ayrshire, making sure that the frail small figure of Maura was protected at his side.

Rory watched as his Dad seemed only moderately surprised as Nessie popped up in the rope noose at the front of the Stag, to power it back for the return journey to Fingal's Cave. He was more surprised at his son's large pet Haggis, that rubbed itself against his legs, looking for a tickle behind the ears! Nessie turned the Stag as Rory thanked Ben for all his help, who hovered high above, and then watched him fly off to go back to his own time and place.

The storm was stronger now, and Rory saw that the abandoned longboats not required by the free slaves were being blown towards the Ayrshire coast. The nearest ones had already been recovered by the fleeing Viking force, some who were attempting to rescue their comrades, to escape home.

'They would have to row them and see what it was like to be a slave, cold, tired and hungry,' Rory thought.

King Haakon Haakonsson had been deprived of the ancient treasure that he had searched for with the fabled cup of life which was rumoured to be from King Solomon's Temple and was brought to Scotland by the returning Templars. He would never know how close he was to getting his hands on it, but he had seen the monster and what it could do. He shouted instructions to the galley crew and he ran or rowed for his life away from it!

The Vikings had now been well defeated and history would record that they would never return to this part of Scotland or tell the real reason why!

Rory planted his feet on the Stag letting the power of the Hagpipe flow through the boards and along the rope into Nessie. He had some time now to catch up with his Dad as they travelled back to Fingal's Cave. His Dad although weak had more questions about Rory and his Mum Mary than Rory had about him, which seemed to strengthen him along with some of the Hagpipe power flowing through the ship. He did not know what to say about his Mum without upsetting his Dad and he told him how they had ended up residing at Urquhart Castle.

Although weak, his Dad looked forward to having a word with John Grant who he now knew was responsible for his disappearance. Rory spoke about how he remade the sword which his Dad was very interested in and he was able to hold it easily when Rory handed it to him. Rory told him about his initiation the previous night or in the future if you went by the date which they laughed at.

Rory was surprised when his Dad shook his hand and exchanged the word and he turned out to be his brother as well as his father!

They arrived back at Fingal's Cave and Rory blew the Hagpipe and activated the portal which glowed yellow/orange as he thought of returning to the same time that he had left at the cave in Urquhart Castle. Nessie pulled the Stag into Fingal's Cave and they emerged into Loch Ness. It was night time and only minutes had passed since they had left.

Nessie towed the Stag to the pier at the water gate and the ship was berthed the easiest way, face in. That would give Captain Roddy something to think about tomorrow! Rory talked his Dad into returning to the refectory with him to get cleaned up, and to get a good feed before seeing his wife.

He didn't want to wait but he also wanted to be more presentable when he saw her so as not to distress her with his condition. Rory thanked Nessie for all her help and she swam back into Loch Ness for a spot of dinner as well. Rory walked with his Dad and stopped at the foundry on the way to the refectory, and he quickly released him from the manacles still attached to his wrists and his ankles. He noticed the red weals where they had been rubbing against his skin for so many years which would never go away. Rory ran up to his room and got his spare highland kilt which would fit his Dad perfectly.

They carried on walking to the refectory. Both were unaware of Hag walking beside them and they totally accepted her presence as normal. Unfortunately, not everyone else felt the same, and it was a clear path all the way through the castle. The party was just starting to warm up when Rory, his Dad and Hag walked into the refectory.

The whisky had just restored the nerves of the four warriors who had captured Hag, and then they saw her walk in the front door to a stunned silence, at Rory's quick return. It was another quick exit as they ran for their lives seeing Hag's smiling face. Everyone including Hag in Rory's head, burst out laughing again at the 'brave' Warriors.

Abbot MacCallum quickly took charge and arranged for a hot bath, food and drink for Rory's Dad who was given a very warm reception. He had to be quite forceful to get him away from the greeting crowd. Once he was cared for, the Abbot joined Rory who experienced plenty of privacy thanks to Hag sitting at his ankles keeping the merely curious from disturbing them as they spoke with Rory updating him on his newest adventure!

CHAPTER 15

Consequences

Ruaidri returned wearing Rory's spare kilt which hung on his skinny frame. He was euphoric at being back in his own time and reunited with his son, who he was very proud of. Despite the lack of good food for the last thirteen years and the extreme physical labour that he had endured, he was in remarkably good health.

He knew the story of the Great One, as he was a Brother of H.A.G.I and he had suspected that his son would be fulfilling this prophesy being the seventh Mac Sween to possess the Hagpipe. He was looking forward to seeing his wife Mary, and he planned his revenge on John Grant. Rory had told him that she had born him a son, young Johnny, but the only grudge that he had was with John Grant. It was not the boy's fault, and all the blame resided at the door of his father, who had manip- ulated his way into his wife's life.

Ruaidri had not had a whisky for the duration of his captivity, and the first one went straight to his head. Every visiting warrior and person present wanted to shake his hand, and hear his story. Being a brother to all of them made this a night to remember, and with the events of the coming of the Great One, they all had very special reports to make when they returned to their own Temple Lodges. Whether they would be believed was another matter!

Abbot MacCallum had arranged quarters for Ruaidri in the nearby monastery, in the softest most comfortable bed that he could find. This was just as well, as come whisky number five he passed out into a deep sleep, no matter how hard he tried to stay awake.

The Constable of the Keep, John Gregg, had been very busy since the return of Rory and Ruaidri. He visited Laird John Grant in his quarters in the castle and found him sober for a change. He had heard the excited reports of the events in the castle, and he was a very worried man. The Constable reported that even he could not protect him from Ruaidri, when he came to enact his revenge on him.

The whole castle was behind him after they had heard what he had done, and no one would support the Laird. John Gregg really didn't want to protect him in any case, as he now realised that he had been duped (used/misled) by him, all those years ago, when he took Mary away from Ruaidri. He barely resisted the urge to take some revenge himself!

He didn't have to give the coward John Grant much encouragement for him to hurriedly collect his valuables and get on a horse and flee to his estate in Glen Moriston (Gaelic Gleann Moireasdan), a few hours ride away, to come up with a plan for his future survival. He was already working on this, and he knew that the old witch who he allowed to live on the estate would help him.

Magic was at work with the return of the husband of Mary, and he would make sure that it wouldn't be for long. He would need magic to combat magic and to regain control of Urquhart Castle. He rubbed the crystal charm on the long chain around his neck. He was lucky, the Talisman was still working, giving him the circumstances to allow him to escape. Ruaidri was sound asleep, and he would see to it that the sleep would be permanent!

The castle in the absence of the Laird fell under the Stewardship of the Constable, who in any case, would make a far better job of it. He was well liked and respected not feared.

Rory was waiting in the monastery outside his father's room the next day for him to awaken, when Granny Grant came to see him. She had received a report from Esther, who had been at Mary's bedside all night. Esther was very worried about Rory's Mum and had a messenger contact Granny Grant to come and see her. Mary had taken a turn for the worse overnight, following all the excitement and exertion of Rory's birthday, and had gone to her bed early the previous night.

Rory accompanied Granny Grant to his Mum's room, and he noticed that she was very sallow-skinned and was making a rattling noise as she breathed, and passed in and out of consciousness. No matter how much he tried to coax her he couldn't get his Mum to eat or drink. Granny was very worried, and she said that the bone disease had spread to the rest of her body, and that she did not think that she would have long to live, as she had the death rattle.

Rory was distraught, but he knew that he had to stay strong for his Dad, and he was worried that he would not wake up in time to see his Mum, before she died. He ran back to the monastery to see if his father was up, and found him awake and fully clothed. He was desperate to see his wife Mary. Rory tried to forewarn his Dad for what he was about to see, and he explained to him that his Mum had taken a turn for the worse overnight, trying to prepare him for his reunion with her.

His Dad was very determined to see her, and he pushed past Rory in a hurry to go and see his wife. He appeared to have realised by Rory's actions that time was of the essence, and he regretted not going straight to see her, when he had arrived home. He had seen a great deal of death at the hands of the Vikings, and wanted to be there at the end, and hold his living wife one last time.

They arrived at her room in the Grant Tower, but nothing could prepare them for the deterioration in Mary's health. Ruaidri rushed to her side, taking her right hand, calling her name. She was very frail, but she regained semi-consciousness, opening her eyes.

She spoke saying, "Ruaidri is that you? Have you come for me?" thinking that he was a spirit coming to take her to the next life.

Rory went to his mother's left side with tears welling in his eyes, and he took her left hand, wishing nothing more in his life than for her to be well, as his Father took her right hand, unable to hold back the tears that were streaming down his face.

The Hagpipe at this time, went hot against Rory's chest and his skin began to glow white. It intensified and passed down his left hand into his Mothers left hand. It also illuminated with the same light which continued to move up her arm and across her chest and down her right arm into his Dad's right hand. He too began to shine in the white light, until all three of them were glowing head to foot, bathed in it. A feeling of great peace and health came over all three of them, and it held them in a trance for what seemed like an eternity. Time appeared to stand still until abruptly the Hagpipe went cold against Rory's chest, and the light went out.

Rory looked at his Mum and his Dad both fully conscious. They both were the picture of vibrant good health!

His parents sat gazing into one another's eyes in silence, in total disbelief at being reunited. His Mum was cured and the cancer which had affected her was gone! As both cuddled, Rory noticed that the red weals that had been on his Dad's wrists and ankles were no longer visible. They too had been eradicated in the healing light, and he too was restored to full health!

Rory left the room to give his parents time alone to get reacquainted, and as he left, looking backwards at them, he walked into Heather, who stood waiting outside the door. She looked into the room to see his Mum unbelievably restored to full health, and she noticed how Rory also seemed calmer and different in some way.

Rory looked at Heather and he knew what he wanted just now, and it was her. He put his hand in his sporran removing something which he concealed in his right palm and he knelt in front of Heather so that they were face to face. Rory took hold of her left hand in his and placed the silver Celtic ring which fitted perfectly, on her index finger with his right. The ring could have been made especially for her, and Rory knew that the circular Celtic design on it, spelt 'Love'!

Heather was dumbstruck. all her dreams had come true in one day. They both embraced as a fire lit inside Rory, as hidden emotions that he had only vaguely experienced before, became a cauldron of heat multiplied sixteen-fold by the power of the Hagpipe. He lost all inhibitions, as he became engulfed in a red fire this time, as he stood-up, lifting Heather from the ground and he carried her to his old secluded bedroom in the Grant Tower.

Rory knew now the reason now why his Father had kept the Hagpipe in its box when he was with his Mother, as extreme emotions were also multiplied by its power. He became a feral primeval beast behaving like a wild mating Haggis, and he was unable to control the emotions coursing through the fire in his blood.

Heather was also engulfed in the fire emitting from Rory as he lifted her. She too had no control over herself, as her deep feelings of love for Rory surged to the surface. Heather had dreamt of this very moment when Rory would be hers for years, and any consideration of their actions were totally ignored and did not even register in her conscious mind in the heat of this passion engulfing her.

The fire within them blazed to a peak, until their emotions were spent, and eventually subsided, as they diffused into their bones and slowly went out. Both Rory and Heather were left exhausted, and bathed in a warm glow as they rested. After a while, they dressed and guiltily walked hand in hand to the main castle kitchen for some breakfast, and to break almost all of the good news to Heather's Mum.

Moira Paterson Cooper the Head Cook was hard at work organising the new batch of young scullery maids, who had replaced the older girls, who had left to get married or who had been promoted to more senior posts in the castle. She had a great deal of life experience, and immediately noticed the change in Heather and Rory, as they walked in, smiling at one another, and holding hands. Any perceptions that she had had about the couple were quickly forgotten, as Heather broke the good news to her Mum of their engagement and the curing of Rory's Mum. She joined in their celebrations, and was swept up into the excitement exuding from the happy couple, as they planned a celebration party to inform all the castle of the miracle healing of Mary, and to announce their engagement.

Rory's Father Ruaidri was disappointed at not having revenge on John Grant, after he found out that he had fled the castle, but the feeling of peace still endured in him, as he remained entwined in the arms of his wife, who he promised would never be separated from again. He felt the best thing for him and for Mary would be to forgive John Grant, and to concentrate on living for now and not to spend the rest of his life hunting him down. He spent hours talking to Mary about their future, and he still wanted to return and regain his own estate at Sween Castle.

But a flash of hate remained in the back of Ruaidri's head and if John Grant ever crossed his path again, he was pretty sure how he would react!

Young Johnny, now his stepson, was a problem. They sat down with him, and discussed his future. Johnny did not want to leave Urquhart Castle, which caused difficulty, and they sought advice on how to resolve it. The Abbot Malcolm MacCallum said that he would continue to educate him, and that he would be his guardian if he stayed. The Constable would be his protector and steward of the castle and the estate, until he was old enough to take control of it.

Abbot MacCallum was very helpful, and used his influence and the inter-doo-net system, sending messages to Edinburgh. He convinced the authorities that the true heir of Sween Castle had been traced. Ruaidri Mac Sween would be retaking control of his own estate from the descendants of John Menteith, who had retained it illegally following the first battle of Independence when Scottish rule was restored.

The Scottish Government replied that they would not become involved in this civil matter! They did however confirm that the Scottish Army would not be despatched to aid the descendant of Menteith the treacherous, or the Clan Mac Sween. The authorities would be retaining a neutral position on this matter!

The petition to them by Ruaidri Mac Sween was aided by a letter of support from Eoin MacDonald, the Lord of Skye and Torquil MacLeod, the Lord of Lewis and Harris. This was only after a few doos[39] from Rory's pal Angus

---

39 'Doos' slang term for pigeons.

and his wife Esther were sent back to their homes. It had nothing to do with the change of power in the area with all three Clans of MacDonald, MacLeod and Mac Sween forming an alliance, when Clan Mac Sween regained control of their historic adjoining estates. Clan Mac Sween would be a powerful Ally, especially as they had the Loch Ness Monster in their arsenal of weapons!

The Scottish Government did not want to upset the formidable Lords of the Isles, who were left alone to control their own areas. All Ruaidri had to do was to take the castle and to evict the tenant who squatted there, who would not be happy at being forced to leave. He would need the help of his son Rory and his "Friends" to do this. No Problem?

CHAPTER 16

Iona's Return

Rory informed his Dad that he had promised Saint Columba that he would visit him after his rescue, and that he would help retake Sween Castle when he came back.

Captain Roddy had promised to supply aid from the Lord of Lewis his brother Torquil MacLeod, as had Eoin the Lord of Skye, following coaxing from his son Angus, Rory's pal.

Word had spread quickly via the Brotherhood of the Warriors of H.A.G.I, who were secretly integrated at all the castles and Clans, and would do anything to be on good terms with the Great One!

A few days later, after Rory's initiation, the castle population was still getting used to the sight of him walking about with a huge Haggis at his heel.

The younger children who showed no fear were the first to approach Hag, and fed her scraps of food.

The parents were concerned that they were going to be the food, but seeing Hag, lying on her back, being tickled by the children and playing with them, soon convinced them that she was harmless.

Hag enjoyed their company, as well as receiving so much love and attention.

Captain Roddy was still scratching his head as to how his ship had been turned and was facing the wrong way in its berth at the quay.

Rory left him to wonder about it, laughing at the puzzled look on his face.

Rory's control of the three great beasts had become common knowledge, especially as everyone saw his control over Hag and Captain Roddy would soon figure out who had borrowed his ship.

Rory walked to the pier with Hag at his left heel, as strangers visiting the castle quickly got out of his way, as the locals smiled at their terror-struck faces, on seeing the huge Haggis approaching them.

He did not bother to say any goodbyes, as he planned to return to the same time as when he had left so no one would even notice that he had been gone.

He climbed down into the rowing boat that was still tied there, as Hag stretched out her wings, and flew down with rapid beats of them, like a bee, to join him.

Rory looked out to the loch and sent out a mental call to Nessie asking if she was there.

A few seconds later her smiling face with sharp teeth emerged on her long neck, out of the Loch beside him.

He heard her greeting in his head, as he asked her politely if she would pull the rowing boat to Iona.

She replied that she would love to go on a trip, and put her head up through the noose on the long rope that Rory had thrown onto the water.

Nessie towed the boat back to the cave below the castle, and Rory blew his Hagpipe visualizing Saint Columba in 570 AD, in the monastery, in Iona and Fingal's Cave.

The trip was further back in time and the Portal was a crimson colour as they passed through it, to emerge into a calm sea outside Fingal's Cave.

Fortunately, it was a calm summer's day like the one when Rory had left.

It was a very pleasant boat ride over to the pier at Iona Abbey, for his appointment with Saint Columba.[40]

---

40 Saint Columba was born in the country of Donegal in Ireland, in the year 521, and was connected both on his father's and on his mother's side with the Irish royal family and could have been an Irish King if he wished instead of a Priest. He decided on the latter and was carefully educated for the priesthood. After he had finished his ecclesiastical studies he founded Monasteries in various parts of Ireland. The year of his departure from Ireland is, on good authority, ascertained to have been 563 AD, and it is generally said that he fled to save his life on account of a feud with his relations. It is believed that the love of God and of his Brethren was a sufficient motive for entering on the great work to which he was called. His immediate objects were the instruction of the subjects of Conal, King of the British Scots, and the conversion of their neighbours the "Heathen Picts of the North". When Columba was forty-two years of age, he arrived among his kindred on the shores of Argyle at Southend on the Mull of Kintyre. He immediately set to fix on a suitable site for a monastery. This would be erected as his base to issue forth his apostolic missionaries destined to assist him in the work of conversion, and as a training facility to educate the youth set apart for the Holy Ministry. Saint Columba espied a solitary isle lying apart from the rest of the Hebridean group, near the south-west angle of Mull. It was then known by the simple name I. It was Latinized by the monks into Iova or Iona, and was again honoured with the name of I-columb-cil becoming known as the Island of Saint Columba of the Church. This island was presented to Columba by Conal, who was then King of the Christian Scots of Argyle, in order that he might erect thereon a monastery for the residence of himself and his disciples. This islet was the perfect location for the Abbey during such barbarous times. Excerpt from Wikipedia and www.southendargyll.org.uk.

A forty-nine-year-old Saint Columba stood on the shore looking over the sea towards Fingal's Cave. He had just completed a new entry into the book he recorded his premonitions in, and it was unfolding itself in real time before his eyes. A large rowing boat approached from the cave without being rowed. Standing in the middle of it was a giant of a man dressed in a full highland kilt, with a sword on his back, with shoulder length red hair blowing in the wind behind him.

An ugly monster of an animal was standing at the front of it, looking into the water. It was like no other creature he had ever seen before. There were no obvious signs as to how the boat was being propelled towards him, and it looked as if an invisible finger pulled it along. The rowing boat coasted towards the shore, where the tall muscular occupant jumped from it in a mighty leap to the pier, and pulled the retaining rope up from the water and secured it. He then turned and looked back at the sea as if thanking it.

Unknown to Saint Columba, Rory was sending a mental thank you to a submerged Nessie, who replied saying that she was going to do some fishing for lunch. As he turned to face him, Saint Columba was white in the face with fear, staring at the ferocious looking full-size Haggis, now sitting peacefully in the rowing boat, showing its sharp teeth and its enormous tusks at him. If he was this shocked at seeing Hag smiling at him, it was just as well that Rory had asked Nessie to stay submerged and out of sight.

Rory explained to Saint Columba that Hag was his pet Haggis, as if this was a normal occurrence, and he explained that she was quite friendly. Saint Columba did not seem convinced about this, and Rory said that she would remain in the boat when they went to talk, which seemed to calm his nerves. Both walked up the path to the newly constructed monastery building, talking as they went.

Rory explained that he had met him before when he was a little boy, but this meant very little to him, as in his life experience this had not happened yet.

'This is going to get very complicated,' Rory thought. He would need a common reference point to convince him.

They entered the monastery and went to Saint Columba's study which was lined with books in shelves along the walls. Sitting on top of his large oak desk was the book of Saint Columba, open at the picture of Rory arriving at Iona.

Rory put his hand inside his plaid and removed the special book given to him by Abbot MacCallum, and he opened it to the same page, and gave it to Saint Columba. He was shocked with realization and he sat down at his desk, flicking through the pages and comparing them with his book of images and dates.

"You have some pages missing," he said, after a short time.

He opened the pages to a double entry in his book which he turned around on the desk for Rory to look at.

Rory looked at an image of himself. He was now in a dark looking cellar like cavern, tied to a rope being lowered down towards a six-foot-long wooden box with the red cross of Saint John stamped on it. The rope dangled from a hole in the roof where sunlight streamed in illuminating him and the box.

Saint Columba stared at the picture and at Rory and then he said, "I don't know how this is possible, but you are destined to recover the Grail Box."

Rory was lost, and he asked what the Grail Box was? Saint Columba seemed taken back at Rory's ignorance and he explained. The Grail Box was a six foot by three-foot box made from the Cross that Jesus was crucified on. It was made in the three days of darkness following his death, when the world was in despair at the realization of what they had done. It was made to retain all the artefacts of his life and all religious treasures.

It is reported to contain his shroud and the folded napkin that had been over his face which had been recovered from his tomb on his resurrection. It also contains all the old testaments and all the religious scrolls and texts recorded along with the stone plaques carved with the Ten Commandments which Moses had received. The most important artefact in the box is the Grail Cup. It is a wooden cup which was used at the Last Supper and had collected the blood of Christ, as he died on the Cross. It was made from the same Acacia Tree that was used to make the Crucifixion Cross, which in turn, was used to make the Grail Box.

It is the only thing that could contain the potent blood of Christ, because it was made from the same Holy Acacia Wood and had been blessed by him at the Last Supper. It is rumoured now that if anyone were to drink from the cup, they would be blessed with eternal life!

Saint Columba explained that the Grail Box was the greatest prize of the religious world and the person who has it would be able to communicate with God.

He said, "This power cannot fall into the wrong hands or the whole future of mankind would be at stake! It can only be handled by the purified, or great danger would befall that person."

Rory was taken aback, but the proof was in front of him. He was to recover the Grail Box.

Saint Columba continued, "The Apostle Saint John the Evangelist had the Grail Box hidden to protect it, and founded a mystic religious group to keep it that way. Only with their assistance will you be able to recover it." He showed Rory another picture of a Monk receiving a vision from an angel.

"Once you have recovered the Grail Box, you must take it to Saint Winning, who will build an Abbey in Ayrshire, following a vision from God, to keep it safe for evermore. How you are going to achieve this I don't know, but you must have abilities I cannot comprehend to be able to travel through time, similar to the abilities I have that allow me to see what is ordained, and record it in my book."

He turned the pages to the first vision that he had recorded and he stated, "I did not always have this gift." He told Rory how God had given it to him.

"When I was forty-two I travelled with my disciples from County Donegal on the East Coast of Ireland, around the North Coast westward towards Scotland. At this time an evil ill storm blew up from the otherwise calm sea, and it was intent on sinking my ship. I was thrown from side to side across the deck, and I lost my sandals, holding onto the mast, praying to God for help. A miracle occurred and the whole ship was bathed in a blinding white light we were all unable to see. I felt the ship being lifted out of the sea as if by an invisible hand. The whole ship was encased in a bubble of calm, with no wind or drop of rain hitting the decks. It was carried to the sandy shore at Southend, on the Mull of Kintyre which was the nearest point on the Scottish shore to Ireland. I felt the ship moving through the air above the sixty-foot waves and the beach below, and landing on a flat shelf of rock below a hundred-foot overhanging rock wall."

Saint Columba continued, "As I climbed off the ship, and dropped to the ground, the light went out as a jolt of power shot though my body and out of my feet, which sank into the ground. It was at then that I had my first premonition."

He showed Rory the first entry in his book of a ship being carried on three large humps, above huge waves towards the shore.

Rory recognised the humps of Nessie immediately, holding up the ship, as Saint Columba carried on with his story.

"On looking down at my feet, I saw that they had not sunk into soft earth as I thought, but into rock. I pulled them free, leaving my footprints there[41]. I looked around and I saw that the rest of the crew and the disciples had climbed from the ship, and were uninjured. Some were drinking at a well set into the rock face nearby. An old hermit of a man approached me who gave his name as Stan, who said that he was the Wise Man of the ancient volcanic Keil Cave."[42]

Saint Columba continued, "He took us all to his nearby large dry cave, set in the cliff face, where a large fire was burning at its centre. We then prayed, thanking God for our deliverance from the evil that had attacked us. Since then I have been recording images which nearly all contain you! I will record an index in my book instructing my descendants to assist you as best as they can without question, starting with Saint Winning."

Rory was intrigued by this story and he knew that as soon as he left that he would have to ensure that it came true, or the Book of Saint Columba would never be written!

He had a lot to think about and to do, before he started to reclaim the estate of his father and Clan Mac Sween, which included Sween Castle, Lochranza Castle on the Isle of Arran and the monastery of Kilwinning, where

---

41 The footprints of Saint Columba can still be seen to this day at this location in Southend and are reported to have been used in the inauguration of Scottish Kings who had promised to follow in the footsteps of their ancestors.
42 Keills is a stack of agglomerate which is fragments of exploded lava in limestone.

Saint Winning would be. Everything was back to front, but it must all be related. He would just do what he had done before, and follow the path in front of him until it all fell into place, but first he had to save Saint Columba!

Both Rory and Saint Columba walked back to the pier, where a very excited Hag jumped from the boat and ran to Rory to be petted. This gave Saint Columba quite a stir, until he saw Hag roll on her back to get her belly tickled. The both got back into the rowing boat with Rory throwing the retaining rope into the water.

Saint Columba watched as Rory stood in the middle of the boat with his left hand over his heart, unknown to him holding his Hagpipe. His feet seemed rooted to the boat's planks as the Haggis again stood at its front, looking into the sea as her friend Nessie slipped her neck through the noose. The rowing boat smoothly pulled away from the pier and gathered speed towards Fingal's Cave.

Saint Columba scratched his head, oblivious as to what had powered the boat, as he said a silent prayer for Rory's mission.

'This was a very unusual young man,' he thought, with Godlike abilities that he could not understand. He thought, 'If anyone could save the world he could,' as he saw a yellow glow flash at the entrance to Fingal's Cave as the boat disappeared!

Rory jumped from the rowing boat onto a rocky shelf within Fingal's Cave, and pulled it from the water, still with Hag standing at its front. He spoke to Nessie, and he asked her if she was willing to help him some more.

Hag was listening to the telepathic conversation between them as Rory mentally explained how he had to go further back into the past to save Saint Columba.

Nessie was willing to help, but Hag would have to stay with the rowing boat until they returned. Hag was quite happy to stay, and she had spotted a few rats running about that she was keen to tidy up. Rory walked to the edge of the shelf and climbed onto the back of Nessie's long extended neck. As soon as they made contact, a waterproof bubble enclosed Nessie's head and neck and Rory, as the Hagpipe glowed with a white light and a warm heat.

He was warm and dry, and Nessie was filled with the power of the Hagpipe. Her strength and her speed were multiplied by Rory's age, and a full-grown Nessie with that natural power multiplied sixteen times was awesome. She relished the extra strength and she was giddy at its intoxicating affect. He was sure even if Nessie submerged that he would stay dry and be able to breathe, similarly to the effect that he had had, travelling with Ben the Eagle, at great heights all those years before.[43]

Rory raised the Hagpipe to his mouth with his left hand, and blew it, visualising the picture in the book of Saint Columba and of his trip to Scotland. The entrance to Fingal's Cave was illuminated with an orange/yellow light, as Nessie swam through it, back out to sea. They

---

43 Refer to Book 1: Rory Mac Sween and the Secrets of Urquhart Castle.

had travelled only a few years further into the past, and surprisingly to Rory, the sea was still calm, with no sign of a storm anywhere.

Nessie picked up speed and swam south towards the Mull of Kintyre, with Rory sitting comfortably on her neck, leaning against her first hump, out of the water, enjoying the ride. She could swim a lot faster when not towing a ship and she enjoyed herself with this super power coursing through her body.

It was a very short journey past the Islands of Colonsay and Jura with the Mull of Kintyre on the West Coast, and Ireland facing them on the right. Rory asked Nessie to come to a halt as he scanned the horizon with his Hagpipe enhanced sight. In the distance he saw a ship in the evening sunshine pass the north of Ireland, travelling towards the Mull of Kintyre. The sea was still calm and the sky was clear, with no sign of a storm.

Rory felt it before he saw it, the blackness behind the ship. It was pure evil, and it was emitting its malevolence towards the ship. This was not a natural storm brewing and it was being controlled by someone or something with great power!

At no previous time had Rory felt challenged like this, by a force that he could not see. He instinctively felt that this was an attempt to change history. If Saint Columba was killed and stopped from coming to Scotland everything would change. No Christianity in Scotland, no Book of Saint Columba, no Hagpipe and no power for Rory to rescue his Father. EVERYTHING would change. He had to act fast; the storm was hitting the ship.

Nessie saw the danger too, and she was already moving towards the ship before Rory could even ask her to.

She was there in seconds with her enhanced speed, diving below the rear of the ship, with Rory still on her neck in his protective bubble. Saint Columba had not exaggerated the danger he had been in with the ship now very close to being sunk! The sky was black above it, with huge waves battering the sides like huge watery hands slapping it from all sides.

The unique abilities of Nessie were now just becoming obvious to Rory as she exhaled air from her humps through her antennas softening them like deflating air bags. She gently rose up below the ship as its hull settled into her humps, like a brick placed into the middle of a soft cushion. The ship rose up out of the water as if in a dry dock, secured by supports at each side.

Rory turned on Nessie's neck, taking hold of the front of the ship with both hands, as he visualized extending his protective bubble around the whole ship. The Hagpipe shone with a blinding white light from his chest, which travelled along his arms and into the ship's hull. The whole ship was engulfed in a white light. The evil force at work could not penetrate the bubble, and not a single raindrop or puff of air touched the decks of the ship.

Nessie swam for the coast of the Mull of Kintyre, towards a red light pulsing above the shore, as the storm swelled the ocean below her. The sea became a wave of gigantic proportions, which was intent on battering her and the ship onto the rocks above the beach, near the light. Nessie realised what was happening, and reversed her forward momentum as she closed in on the coast, raising the front of the ship up in the air. She spoke to Rory, asking him to push the ship up in the air at the same time, as she quickly fully inflated her humps with a sharp intake of air.

The ship was punched upwards off Nessie's back as Rory put all his strength into his arms throwing and guiding the ship towards the shore. It flew through the air sixty feet above the beach, landing parallel with the wave and flat on its hull, on a rocky shelf above the crashing waves battering the rocks below. Nessie reversed back into the sea as Rory turned, hugging her neck thanking her.

Saint Columba was safe!

The storm howled a final protest of frustration, which echoed in the air at being thwarted and denied of its prize. The ill winds ceased as quickly as they had started, with the clouds dissipating, letting the rays of the sun break through, illuminating the sea which calmed to its normal flow.

Rory resumed his original position on Nessie's neck and he looked towards the shore. He saw a flash as Saint Columba stepped from the ship and earthed the remaining Hagpipe power from the protective bubble through his body into the ground, leaving the impression of his feet on a large boulder, level with the right side of the ship.[44].

---

44 The local cover story told to tourist finding them is that they were carved by a Stonemason.

Saint Columba stood with his feet sunk into the rock, as if standing in soft mud, as he experienced his first premonition seeing Nessie carrying the ship with Rory holding its front. History was back on course. As Rory watched from the sea, he looked for any signs of the attacker. The only other person he could see who stood on the coast illuminated by a huge red bonfire glowing out of a cave behind him was a slim built, grey-haired old man dressed in rags like a hermit.

'He must be Stan the Wise Man who had helped Saint Columba,' Rory thought. 'It was lucky that he had a big fire emitting light[45] so that we could see the coast.'

Rory felt that the evil in the air was gone. He did not know of the carved pentagram on the rocky floor of Keil Cave, below the ash of the bonfire! This cave was at the end of the lay line leading back to Argyll and Kilmartin Glen, where he was attacked on Ben the Eagle as a child. It was the focal point of the immense evil power which had now been dispersed.

Saint Columba would build his first Chapel a mile to the west of this spot at Kilcolmkill, with the patronage of the MacDonald Lord of the Isles. He was safe at present, surrounded by his fellow fighting Monks, and he literally had his foothold in Scotland.

Rory and Nessie turned, and she speedily swam back to Fingal's Cave, to reunite with Hag to uplift her and the boat, for the trip back to Urquhart Castle. He was

---

45 Like an early lighthouse.

deep in thought during the journey about what he still had to do to restore his birthright and the MSween's family estate.

'What else?' he thought. 'Oh yes and I've got to recover the Grail Box and save the World! No pressure then! But who or what is trying to stop me?'

CHAPTER 17

Preparations

Nessie towed the rowing boat back into Fingal's Cave where a very excited Hag was patiently waiting for their return. She had been very busy whilst they were away, and there was not a rat in sight as she stood with a large swollen belly. She struggled to get back into the rowing boat with her uneven legs and to get a grip on the slippery ruddy marble rock surface. Every noise that she made vibrated around the basaltic pillars reaching up to the cathedral-like roof of the cave.

Rory was still in awe of the beauty and the power of the place, and wondered how it could have been made. Its existence could not be a random coincidence, and he felt that some powerful superior being must have created it, as he could feel the connection to the earth and the lay lines vibrating through every pillar surrounding him.

He helped Hag aboard, petting her as he heard in her voice the delight at his return, as she spoke to him, telepathically. A bond that could not be broken had formed between all three of them; the mythical magical creatures and Rory, with a mental connection between all of them. It was now time to go home and to plan the restoration of the family estates to the Mac Sween's before he considered how to recover the greatest prize known to mankind.

Rory blew his Hagpipe, visualizing the hidden cave below Urquhart Castle at the exact same time he had left. The trip was forward in time and the Portal at the entrance to Fingal's Cave was illuminated in a bright yellow colour. Nessie waited patiently with the rope noose around her neck, connecting her to the rowing boat, and she joined in the conversation with Hag, updating her with their adventure, as she swam towards the cave exit.

Hag took up her usual position at the front of the rowing boat like a mascot, as the Hagpipe power flowed through the planks, rooting her and Rory's feet to the boat, as they passed through the shimmering Portal which tingled against their skin, as they emerged into the cave and calm waters below Urquhart Castle.

Nessie gave the rowing boat a final strong pull, as she slipped her neck from the noose, propelling it towards the sandy beach. The boat sped towards the shore and half-way out of the water onto the sand. She had judged it perfectly and Rory and Hag wouldn't even get their feet wet. Hag jumped from the boat, followed by Rory, who tied it up to the post on the beach as they both sent a mental 'thanks' to Nessie for her help as she turned and swam out of the cave. Everything was as it should be. They walked together to the spiral staircase and back to the temple.

The castle occupants became used to the sight of Rory accompanied by his large pet Haggis walking at his left heel, as they emerged from the building into the castle courtyard. The young children were more empathic than the older ones as they did not know fear, or were corrupted by stories from their parents to keep away from Hag in case she ate them. They rushed to Hag every time they saw her, to pet her, which she just loved. The older ones on seeing this dared one another to do the same, and soon all were petting and playing with this giant of a Haggis.

Rory could sense a feeling of excitement in the air, as he walked past the main castle kitchen. His friends Wee Charlie and Pally Ally appeared from nowhere, with big smiles on their faces, and each took him by the arm, as they propelled Rory into the entrance of the main building, and up the stairs into the Great Hall.

It was full of all his friends, who let out a cheer as he entered, with Heather running to him and jumping into his arms.

It was an engagement party!

Word travelled very quickly in the confines of the castle. Rory saw his healthy Mum and his Dad smiling at one another, and holding hands, accompanied by his brother Johnny. Standing beaming at him, next to his future in-laws Moira and Hamish Cooper was a smiling Abbott MacCallum and Pooie Doo (Father Doogan) standing, holding empty tankards, waiting for the beer barrel to be tapped (opened).

A queue soon formed, with Angus and his wife Esther at the front, holding baby Eoin, waiting to congratulate Rory and Heather. Angus was exceptionally pleased that Rory would soon be experiencing married Bliss, and he looked forward to his realisation of what that would really entail.

Heather had already collected a great deal of engagement presents from all the guests, with wedding plans firmly on her mind, and she and Esther were soon huddled together as thick as thieves, talking about wedding dresses with Esther staking her place as chief bridesmaid, and picking-out what she would wear to make sure that she did not look like a pudding in the bridesmaid dress like Martha had, at her wedding (she had worn a pink dress and she looked like a pink, wobbly blancmange pudding).

Moira and Hamish were equally pleased at the announcement, which had been expected but maybe not so soon. Hamish, the new father of a daughter, was not quite so excited as he would have to pay for the wedding and going by the crowd in the Great Hall, it was going to be a very big expensive one!

Heather was positively glowing, and Rory noticed that Granny Grant stood alone in the far corner of the Hall. She was studying Heather, and she looked very deep in thought! Rory did not have time to consider this, as Jimmy Black and Gordon Grant arrived, pushing a large barrel of beer and receiving another loud cheer from the surrounding guests. They were closely followed into the Hall by Murdo Hands the Stableman, aided by his former apprentice Wee Charlie, both pushing two smaller barrels of whisky to an even louder cheer. You don't need much of an excuse in the Highlands to have a party, and this was a day to really celebrate. It wasn't every day that you have a miracle cure and an engagement!

Rory eventually found time to sit down, as Hag curled up at his feet below the table. Hag behaved a bit strangely as well. She had walked up to Heather, and sniffed the air around her. He mentally asked her what she was doing, but she was very evasive, and she said that it was just Haggis stuff!

Rory's Dad came up to him at this time, with a pint of the new brew that Gordon and Jimmy had brought in. The beer was Dark Ruby Red Ale, and was strong at 8.9% abv. Jimmy and Gordon had decided to name it 'Miracle', after the miracle cure of Rory's Mum. It was already living up to its name, as it was a miracle if you were able to walk straight after three pints of it!

Rory and his Dad spoke about how to regain control of Sween Castle without too much bloodshed. Ruaidri said that he had already sent a trusted fellow brother of H.A.G.I to make discreet enquiries at Sween Castle, among the brothers there and to let them know of his return. He hoped that there would not be too much resistance if they saw a sign that the Great One was on their side.

Rory considered this, and he said that he could ask Nessie to patrol up and down Loch Sween disturbing John De Menteith's shipping which would really agitate them and to have Ben, the great Scottish Eagle regularly circle the castle to scare them as well. His Dad thought that this was a great idea and laughed at what the uninitiated in the castle would think on seeing them.

He wanted to be back in his own castle by Christmas just after the winter equinox, on the twenty second of December. Rory said that he would give his Dad a loan of Hans his Magic Sword which he could handle just as well as his son.[46] He could lead a small force of H.A.G.I

_____

46 Today we know about Genetics giving similar family traits and abilities.

Warriors overland to Sween Castle and he could even borrow Jet his horse.

Rory would ask Ben to fly him to the castle and to drop him off inside it, and he would open the drawbridge and the gate, aided by the Brothers of H.A.G.I within. That way they would not have to ask for aid from their allies, the Lords of Skye the MacDonald's and the Lord of Lewis and Harris the MacLeod's. They did not want to be indebted to them, which they would be if they asked them for help. It would also save a lot of bloodshed which would happen with a full attack on the castle.

Ruaidri thought that this was a great plan and that the only drawback would be the weather, if there was too much heavy snow impeding the journey to Sween Castle. Rory said that he would start constructing a special reinforced enclosed wagon for his Mum to travel in, with wide wheels, so that the snow and the ice would not be a problem. The plan was agreed-on, and Rory felt slightly sorry for the innocents in Sween Castle who were about to be visited by Nessie and Ben!

Time passed quickly as Autumn approached, along with reports from Sween Castle of the terror that Nessie and Ben inflicted on the local population who thought that the castle was cursed, and that the laird Sir John De Menteith the younger was receiving his just reward for his ancestor's betrayal of William Wallace[47].

---

47 See the film Braveheart.

It was also reported that Menteith was considering retreating to Lochranza Castle on the Isle of Arran, for his own safety. Rory was encouraged by this, and the next time when Ben flew back to report on the number of hostile forces on the ground, he would instruct him to tell Nessie to sink any ships fleeing to Arran.

The coach was almost complete and as December approached, Rory and his Dad received reports that many of the troops loyal to John De Menteith had left the castle and had deserted him. They were scared to remain there, and most of those left were members of the Brotherhood of H.A.G.I. who were feigning loyalty to John De Menteith.

Rory had been preoccupied with all the plans to retake Sween Castle and in making the coach that he had not spent much time in, with his fiancée Heather. He had recovered more than a dozen valuable Haggis Tusks from the Haggis Graveyard, and he had given them to the Abbot, to create a fund for his Mum and Dad at Sween Castle to provide financial security for them.

He had not noticed Heather's weight gain as she had taken to wearing heavy, baggy clothing saying that it was just to keep the winter chill out!

CHAPTER 18

The Twins and the Witch

John Grant was a very bitter man, following his forced evacuation from Urquhart Castle. He was upset at the loss of face, but more so, he missed the power that he had wielded there, and it really hurt him. He still had some spies in the castle and one in particular, who kept him aware of all the events there, and he received regular reports at his only remaining estate in Glen Moriston (Gaelic Gleann Moireasdan).

No one had come to look for him, which surprised him. He had expected Ruaidri Mac Sween to have pursued him to enact revenge and to kill him, and he was unable to understand why he had not done so?

That was what he would have done!

The only saving grace was that young Johnny, his son, would be the laird at Urquhart Castle and when things calmed down and he had disposed of the Mac Sweens he could return and resume control. The first thing that he had to do was to visit the old Witch. He needed powerful magic to defeat his Stepson Rory Mac Sween, who could control the Three Magical Beasts, Nessie, Haggis and the Great Eagle. The Witch still lived in the old stone cottage surrounded by the ancient stone circle, which was hidden in the forest in the middle of the Glen Moriston Estate.

John Grant was not surprised when he found that the witch was expecting him. He was taken aback when he noticed how much the old Hag appeared to look so similar to Granny Grant, as she stood, bent over, supported by a sturdy twisted knotted walking stick with her straggly dirty grey hair. The only difference was the unkempt look and an evil glint in her eye and also the cackle emitting from her mouth, when she laughed on seeing him.

She was very willing to train him in her dark arts, and she made him kneel in the middle of the Pentagram carved in the stone floor of the cottage. She held her Jet Black Crystal above his head, and a black cloud appeared in the air above him, which seemed to feed off the anger and the hatred that emanated from him, which he felt towards the Mac Sween's. The witch cackled with delight as the evil intent that he projected concentrated in the blackness. It solidified and consumed John Grant, and it turned the white crystal that was around his neck black, as he embraced its sinister power!

He felt it soaring through his blood, exhilarating him and it filled him with a potential for great power, and it teased him by giving him a perverse delight that filled him with evil thoughts.

Revenge would be his!

Heather was very worried. She had seen enough pregnant serving girls in the castle to know that she was in deep trouble. She could not understand how she could be so heavily pregnant and soon it would be impossible to hide it. No amount of baggy clothes would help conceal the large bump that she had. She was too far gone to marry Rory now, as she showed a term of pregnancy which indicated that she must have conceived months before his return to the castle. She could not confide in her mother as childbirth outside marriage was taboo, and she would be accused of being unfaithful to Rory with someone else, before his return.

"That is so untrue!" she wailed to herself. She loved Rory and at no time ever had she looked at another man!

Granny Grant spent a lot of her time concealed in her cabin, trying to avoid Heather. Every time she saw her it caused her pain in more ways than one. She could not tell her what was happening as she was physically racked with pain in her abdomen if she got too close to Heather, and Granny Grant knew why! Soon, the events that she dreaded would unfold, and if she did not time it right she would cease to exist!

Final preparations were being put in place for Abbot Malcolm MacCallum and Constable John Gregg to take full control as Guardian and Steward of Urquhart Castle, over young Johnny Grant with Moira Cooper and husband Hamish moving along with Heather, into the Grant Tower to provide a family unit and to care for him.

A dozen of the best warriors who were members of the Brotherhood of H.A.G.I, were assembled at the gates of Urquhart Castle on horseback, along with Rory on his horse Jet. His father and his mother were inside a specially constructed carriage which was laden with their possessions and supplies, both inside and on a roof rack on top of it.

Rory, as planned, had given his Dad his Sword 'Hans', which was in the carriage with him and he would accompany them on Jet for most of the journey, before calling Ben the Eagle. He had not seen Heather for days and he thought she might be avoiding him, and that she was possibly in a huff because he was leaving.

He assumed that she was not happy with him, as he would miss their first Christmas together as a couple, and thereafter he was going away on his quest for the Grail Box. He promised that he would make it up to her, and he had instructed Hag to stay and to protect her when he was away. He didn't have to tell Hag to do this, as she had not left Heather's side for weeks, which come to think of it, was a bit strange!

Rory only knew that he had to go. There was too much depending on him and he had to recover the Grail Box and save the World. He was very upset to leave under the current circumstances but he had no other choice!

The weather was kind to them for the few days, it would hopefully hold until the winter Equinox on the twenty second of December. It was below freezing point, with a clear sky and a layer of ice on the iron-like ground. This was far better than deep snow or watery slush, which would slow them down considerably!

The war party headed by Rory and his Dad, who looked like twins, dressed in identical full Highland dress with their Clan Mac Sween heavy one-piece kilts, set off to recover Sween Castle. Rory rode at the front of the party on his giant Jet-black stallion, along with the twelve mounted warriors. His Dad brought up the rear, in charge of the four horse-drawn, specially reinforced black carriage containing his Mum.

Heather was very sad and confused and she cried as she watched them from the top of the Grant Tower! Hag rubbed against her legs trying to console her. Hag knew that Heather was very pregnant and that she would give birth soon. Heather was unaware as to why she was so pregnant? She did not know that it was because of the magic of the Hagpipe, which had been transferred into her, during the burning lust enhancing emotions she had experienced as she joined in union with Rory, and that it had vastly accelerated her pregnancy!

Granny Grant knew what was happening to Heather. She was magically linked to her, and every emotion that she experienced Granny Grant also experienced, including feeling the pain of Heather's first contraction. Granny Grant was filled with dread at what she knew was to come; it was the twenty second of December, the winter equinox.

It was time!

She stumbled with each contraction that Heather endured, as she walked to the Grant Tower carrying her medicine bag, as a winter snow storm began blowing against her in the strengthening wind.

Heather waited at the entrance to the Grant Tower with a concerned Hag at her ankles looking up at her. She planned to head to the most remote communal privy to get privacy away from her mother. She intended to deliver the baby herself, but was woefully out her depth. Her heart leapt on seeing the frail stooped figure of Granny Grant leaning on a walking stick, carrying her large medicine basket, appearing in front of her through a curtain of white snow.

Another contraction doubled both Heather and Granny Grant over, as she reached her in the doorway. Heather was more concerned for Granny Grant than herself on seeing her. She was young and strong. Granny was old, frail and looked very weak! The contraction passed, and both recovered, panting heavily. Granny dropped her stick and she took Heather by her free right arm, while holding her basket in her left hand and she propelled Heather towards the nearby temple with Hag at their feet. The contractions were fifteen minutes apart, but progressed rapidly as they entered the temple, out of the storm, and made their way to the far wall in the East with the letter G on the wall.

The full super moon of the Winter Equinox forced a beam through a break in the clouds and through the stained-glass windows and illuminated them in the blue colours of the loch and the purple of Saint Columba's robe, as they neared the altar. Hag knew where they were going, and she ran ahead and jumped up on the altar and upwards off it and she pushed the G on the wall with her snout, opening the secret door.

The next contraction came and passed, as Heather and Granny reached the door. A few deep breaths later Granny took a candle from her laden bag and lit it as Hag ran ahead down the spiral staircase, slowly followed by Heather and Granny. Heather did not know where she was going, but she knew that she was being helped, and that was all that mattered to her right then.

Moonlight entered and bounced off the still water in the huge cavern below the castle, as Granny and Heather walked, turning left from the stairs towards the smaller Haggis Graveyard Cave. Hag waited for them and she let out a high-pitched squeal as a white shimmering curtain illuminated its entrance.

The contractions were minutes apart now, and Granny Grant visibly struggled with the pain that she felt, and she was now being supported more by Heather than the other way round. They passed through the curtain of power into the cave, as the interior was illuminated with light from the reflective roof crystals, which fed off the candles' glow. Granny sat, put the candle on a rocky shelf to keep it safe, as she would need her hands. She didn't know how she would find the strength to complete her task, but she had to do it!

Heather looked around and she saw a gleaming mountain of Haggis Tusks next to a large circle of stones on the sandy floor. Granny took a quilt out of her basket and she placed it in the stone circle and she asked Heather to lie down on it.

She had just made it in time as the strongest contraction yet, racked her body, forcing her legs into the air as a concerned Hag cuddled next to her in the circle. Heather looked up at Granny Grant, as the pain coursed through her, looking for help. She was terrified at what she saw! With each pulse of pain Granny flashed in and out of existence!

The Grant Witch and her trainee Warlock John Grant were also busy on this Winter Equinox, making use of the powerful natural forces coming into alignment. Both stood inside the pentagram inside her cottage which was perfectly located in the centre of the stone circle surrounding it. The power built to a peak at midnight, as the witch raised her jet-black crystal above their heads. The pentagram filled with a malevolent black cloud, which emitted from the crystal as a piercing scream vibrated in the air around them, as they vanished!

Heather let out a mighty scream which vibrated around the cave. First one and then another baby was born in quick succession, as two crystals, one Jet Black and the other Pure White fell from the shimmering reflective ceiling into the stone circle, next to the twin girls.

Granny stood transparent like a ghost as she spoke to Hag, "You know what to do, protect them!" as Hag, the twins and the crystals vanished!

CHAPTER 19

Adversaries

Rory and the party had made good time on the journey from Loch Ness, passing Fort William and Oban, and stopping for the night at an Inn and stables in Kilmartin Glen in Argyll, which would be their last rest spot, before continuing to Sween Castle the next day. Rory recognised the area, as he had passed there before carried by Ben when he was a boy. His Hagpipe had been pulsing constantly as they travelled past Dunadd Fort, the ruined stone citadel of the First Kings of Scotland, and the huge stone burial mounds interspersed between large stone circles.

This was a magical ancient place!

Rory left the party asleep as he went out into the bright clear, crisp frozen night lit by a giant full moon. It was in alignment and it shone on the lines of standing stones, populating the Glen like groups of stone people standing in circles. He could feel that something was happening, as he saddled Jet, and left the war party and rode him to a high spot, looking down on the Glen.

It was the winter equinox and midnight was seconds away as Rory felt a surge of power course through him and the Hagpipe next to his chest. The standing stones stood out in front of him in the bright moonlight, and appeared to shimmer and momentarily flash in and out of existence as midnight struck.

A scream rent the air as the stones disappeared and Rory recognised who it belonged to. It was Heather! He had to go back and see if she was all right. He turned Jet towards the nearest stone circle and he rode as fast as he could towards it.

Granny Grant fully materialised into her normal solid form as Hag, the twins and the crystals disappeared. Heather sat up, bewildered at the events that had transpired, and she looked around her for her babies. They were gone, in fact there was no sign that they had even been born! She felt that she had never been pregnant and there was absolutely nothing in her appearance to show she had been.

It was as if it had never happened, but she knew that she had carried them. She gave Granny Grant a confused look and demanded an answer.

Granny explained to Heather she wasn't going mad and that it had happened. Her babies were safe she could confirm that, but she would have to wait to see them. Rory was going to be coming back very soon to see her, and it was imperative that she pretended that all was well, and not to mention what had happened.

They would have to hurry before he arrived, and she should get to her bed before that. She told Heather to come and see her the next day and she would explain it the best way she could.

Rory arrived at the nearest stone circle, which looked like a miniature version of Stonehenge. He jumped off Jet, who was steaming in the cold air, and he instructed him to keep warm and to graze while he was away. He watched as Jet wandered off to a clump of long grass covered in frost, for a bite to eat. Rory walked to the two tallest stone pillars in the circle, and removed the Hagpipe from inside his shirt and gave it a short blow as he visualised the beach outside Hag's cave below Urquhart Castle.

A sparkling white light illuminated between the two monoliths. Rory stepped through it as if walking through a doorway and set foot on the sandy beach. He was back at Urquhart Castle in real time, with the moonlight reflecting off the water in the large cave, from its exit to Loch Ness. With his enhanced sight, he could see that the sand had been recently disturbed by two persons who had stumbled and staggered along it with the obvious distinct ungainly footprints of Hag scattered about. He checked inside Hag's cave which, in real time, was barren and undisturbed, except for a few rats running about.

Rory followed the footprints to the spiral staircase leading to the temple, and up it, pulling the lever opening the secret door set in the east wall, and stepped through it. Rory concentrated and used all his enhanced senses to look for anything unusual, but the temple and the whole castle was quiet, except for some snoring coming from the nearby monastery building.

He went into his stealth mode using his martial arts skills, and silently and invisibly, like a ninja warrior, he left the temple, unseen, and made his way to the Grant Tower. He knew that Heather had moved into his old room, which had been redecorated and refitted with her feather mattress bed, after the lumpy old horsehair one had been destroyed.

He moved like a shadow up the stairs, on alert for whatever it was that had made Heather scream. The noises from the Grant Tower were different from when he stayed there, but they were normal sounds. As he passed the master bedroom, he heard loud snoring from Hamish, and a snort from him as his wife Moira thumped him, making him roll on his side to stop the noise. He had to stifle a laugh at this insight into their life, as he carried on to Heather's room.

Rory silently entered her room like a ghost, and looked down on the slim shape of Heather sleeping peacefully below her sheets. She breathed quietly, and was obviously quite well. There was no sign of Hag which was fortunate, as she would have detected him sneaking about. She was most likely away hunting rats in the dark, looking for a good feed. He looked down at Heather, and felt filled with love for her.

He bent forward and gave her a kiss on her forehead, making up for the one that he had missed giving her, when he had left, days before. Heather squirmed in her bed, smiling as Rory silently, or so he thought, left the room.

'Everything was all right here so where did the scream come from?' Rory asked himself.

The stones were blinking in time, one second, they were in the past where they did not exist, and then they appeared in the present again. He considered that the scream must have come from another point in time, not this one, and that whatever had caused it had not happened yet.

'That must be it,' he thought.

He had never been so wrong!

The new-born baby girls and a ferocious fully-grown Haggis materialised in the same cave below Urquhart Castle many thousands of years in the past, long before the castle was built.

This was even further in the past than when Rory had recovered the broken sword from the Druids. In the stone circle above where the temple now stood, Urquhart Castle was being constructed now by these ancient mystical people, who stood and surrounded the baby girls in Hag's cave, looking at them in wonder. A village of sorts was built along the beach outside with this small cave being the abode of their leader. It had a large bonfire at its rear that allowed the smoke to escape up the small tunnel-like caves at its rear. The cave entrance was secured by wooden panels with a door in the middle.

It was still the middle of winter at the equinox, but Hag's cave was a warm and inviting place, as the leader of these very ancient Druids performed a ritual over a circle of stones in the middle of the cave. At precisely midnight, the crystal roof began to brighten and dim and the babies and Hag appeared in the circle, as a scream rent the air.

The huge Haggis stood over the top of the tiny identical naked girls, except for their different coloured hair, and it appeared to be protecting them, as the shocked Druids looked on. The air went cold as the bonfire in the rear of the cave went black, as two figures; one a small wizened old woman holding a black crystal, and a middle-aged slightly- built, evil looking man appeared in the middle of the flames. The malevolence that emanated from them was palatable, as Hag stared at them growling and challenging them to approach the babies.

This was not lost on the Druid Chief, who could see this as a standoff between good and evil. He held a long staff made from a branch of their holy oak tree. He swung it into the middle of the fire into the black cloud causing the staff to shatter into several pieces. The witch screamed as the forces of good collided with her evil power, causing both to earth like a lightning rod to the ground. The Chief Druid was thrown back in the recoil from these two opposing powers colliding. The scream of the witch continued to vibrate in the air, as she and John Grant disappeared with the flames of the bonfire, burning up the black cloud.

The Chief Druid rose to his feet and looked at the huge Haggis now sitting patiently behind the babies, considering what had just happened. The ceremony he was conducting was because his wife, who stood in shock and had watched this encounter, had just delivered two stillborn baby girls. He had just cremated his first-born children with an almost broken heart in the fire as an offering to his pagan gods.

The gods that had just delivered them back to him!

He walked to the stone circle and he saw two crystals next to the babies, another sign from the Gods! There was one for each child; one crystal was pure white (Bella), in his dialect meaning beautiful, the other (Isa) meaning black. Hag made no movement as he called his Clan Grant wife to him.

She was heavy with milk and in pain from it. She looked down on the two helpless babies who lay on the ground. Her face burst into a huge smile, as she reached down and lifted them to her breasts.

The Chief Druid named his children as the Gods requested, and he watched his smiling wife feed Bella and Isa. It suited them, and they would never be parted from their talismans. He instructed silver chains be attached to the crystals which was quickly carried out by his talented craftsmen. Raven haired Isa had the jet-black crystal placed around her neck with Bella receiving the pure white one over her blonde locks, as the surrounding community of Druids and their families joined this now happy cere-mony, knowing that they all had been blessed.

The ugly monster protecting the babies was another gift from the Gods. It was left to Hag to do as she willed and she willed to stay with the twins, as she moved and lay down at the feet of the Druids wife as she fed them. No one was going to interfere with this magical guardian who had faced down the evil spirits in the fire!

The Grant Witch accompanied by her new Trainee Warlock she called Stan, re-materialised lying on the ground inside the pentagram in her cottage. This new name of John Grant was taken from the last four letters of his surname Grants; his Clan name, as he reversed his behaviour to follow the path of Darkness. Both of them emanated wisps of smoke from their singed clothing and they ached from the powerful recoil that had thrown them back to their own time. Stan felt for his crystal chained around his neck.

He looked at it now with his black evil filled eyes, reflecting the appearance of the pulsating black smoke-filled crystal. Its malevolent power surged through him as he formulated a new plan to stop Saint Columba from ever stepping onto Scottish soil. This would give free reign for evil to be the dominant force and in the process, to change history and give him total control to take revenge on the Mac Sween's.

If only he knew that this plan was doomed and that it had already been thwarted by Rory and Nessie, thanks to the Book of Saint Columba and the Power of the Hagpipe. Stan did not possess the ability to predict events and he was limited to travelling in time via the Lay Line Portals, with the use of his Crystal and only on the dates of the summer and winter equinoxes.

If John Grant alias Stan was angry now he was going to be absolutely furious when his plan failed!

Rory was not the only person out and about on his return to Urquhart Castle. His half-brother Johnny liked to wander about his new realm, checking on it without the Constable's constant presence by his side. He was his father's son, and he hid his feelings well, but he was very envious of Rory and all the power that he had, and he was still fiercely loyal to his natural father. He had started to sleepwalk, and the current dream he was having had pulled him through the castle grounds and into the room above the foundry that Rory had occupied.

Something in the room was calling him to find it. He saw a vision of his Dad calling to him for it to be returned to him. He wanted to help his Dad as he quietly searched the empty room. He was pulled along like a puppet by this eerie call in his dream state, to the wardrobe. It was empty except for a large dark rag, lying on its floor, where his Dad's voice was coming from.

Johnny reached for it, as he was engulfed by the power of the voice repeating, "Yes, Yes," in his head. He picked the rag up and shook it out, holding it up to the bright moonlight streaming through the small roof window.

It was a crimson red robe with a hood and he knew that it had to go to his Dad, as it pulsed, alive with evil intent, in his hands!

CHAPTER 20

Sween Castle

Rory returned silently to the temple and went down the secret stairs to Hag's cave below the castle. He blew the Hagpipe and visualised his return to the Standing Stones and Jet his horse. The cave entrance was illuminated in white sparkling light as he stepped through it back into a cold wintry night and frozen frosty ground. Jet was running around trying to keep warm and he ran to him as he appeared. He was desperate to get back to the warm stables where he had been before Rory came for him. He ran. remembering the way and he was soon being brushed down with a warm blanket on his back.

A busy day awaited Rory as he went to his bed for a few hours before arising with the party, and a big breakfast feed which would be his last before battle commenced. They continued travelling towards Lochgilphead and the Crinan Fault. It had been created four hundred and seventy million years ago when the continental plates collided and the Caledonian Mountain Belt and the NE-SW linear features of the now Argyll were formed. Ireland had broken away from Scotland at that time as the continents drifted apart. The magnetic molten lava of this volcanic upheaval flowed out into the Dolerite sills below ground and created the powerful Lay Lines.

The lava spread all the way to the Mull of Kintyre and Southend where Saint Columba first set foot in Scotland.

The Keills were created at that time which were subsequently used by the Druids, who created the Standing Stones with them. This was a very ancient magical land which had been occupied by man for over seven thousand years.

The party led by Rory on Jet, approached the Crinan Fault which was now an ice rink in places where the water had frozen. It would in the future, become the Crinan Canal used by tourists to sail to the adjoining Lochs and the West Coast Sea, joining the Sound of Jura. The landscape had a rugged beauty but in it lurked a tiny enemy the midge! Only those well-equipped tourists with full body suits and netted headwear would have protection, but no one could escape the nasty annoying bite of the female midge.

As the Crinan Fault was crossed Rory, his Mum and his Dad were home in North Knapdale and currently free of the midge, as they hibernated until springtime. The terrain was rocky and hilly as they joined the single-track road on the left bank of Loch Sween. The surrounding land was very fertile, and the flat spots were ideal for farming, but the major population around them as they travelled was not man, it was sheep. The hills were white with snow and frost, but in the summer, they were white with sheep.

Rory mentally called out to Ben the Great Scottish Eagle, who he could talk telepathically to, in the same way as he could with Nessie and Hag, with the power of the Hagpipe. There was only a short distance to go now to Sween Castle and they would arrive totally unexpectedly. It was insanity to attempt any assault on it in the winter months. An army could be held at bay outside in the summer but would freeze to death before having any reasonable chance of forcing entry into it in the winter.

But times were not normal, as the laird Sir John De Menteith the younger was beginning to realise. He was still in residence being far too scared to leave for Lochranza Castle on the Isle of Arran with the Loch Ness Monster (Nessie) patrolling the Loch outside. She had already sunk two of his Birlinns (ships) as they attempted to leave the Loch for the sea. They were now lying wrecked on the rocks at Kilmory Bay, at the entrance to the Loch.

The crew had returned drookit (soaked) but otherwise uninjured to the castle. Their tale of the monster had shaken all the castle residents many of whom had left to stay with crofting[48] relatives. The houses in the small town outside the castle were occupied by those who had nowhere else to go. The Giant Eagle had everyone too terrified to go outdoors as its visits came at least twice daily. It would swoop down on anyone brave enough to venture outside, causing them to scurry back inside. It was a nightmare even to go to the outside privy and, if you did make it you had better carry a change of underwear.

Ben answered Rory's call almost immediately. He told him that he was having great fun scaring the wee people, watching them run screaming from him. As soon as he

---

48 A Croft is a remote farming cottage with land.

appeared they all hid indoors, so that the warriors could walk up to the castle gates unimpeded. Rory informed his Dad of this who then grabbed Jet's reins and took charge of the band of warriors. He put on the strap holding the magic sword (Hans) over his back and removed the sword, giving it a few trial swings. He could feel its power and it practically handled itself. The war party were very encouraged at this display as no one else could handle the sword and it was a good omen.

The carriage containing Mary would stay a safe distance away until the castle was secured. The band of Warriors of H.A.G.I had all been at Rory's initiation and they knew that he was special, but even they were surprised when he jumped fifty feet into the air and landed on the back of Ben's neck as he swooped down to pick him up. This was the first time for many of them seeing a giant Scottish Eagle and they were all were convinced that they had picked the right side for this fight.

Confidence was very high as they rode towards the castle and down the steep incline towards the gate. Ben was exhilarated as he received the Hagpower from the Hagpipe around Rory's neck as he flew over the Loch. Rory looked down and he saw Nessie on the surface near to the castle docks. No one would be leaving that way. She intimated to him that she was floating there, ready to assist.[49]

Ben flew around the castle and the town several times and he was right. It was deserted. Everyone was terrified

---

49 Similar to standing ready, only on water.

and hiding. He flew back to the top of the castle and Rory dropped from his neck, landing softly on the highest turret. He went into his stealthy martial arts mode, confident that he would not need a weapon to deal with any hostile encounter. He still had his Sgian Dubh in the top of his right sock, should it be required with its Haggis Tusk fragment attached to its handle. The magical properties of the Tusk gave the Sgian Dubh the ability to cut through practically anything.

Rory was right. The loyal fellow Warriors of H.A.G.I within the castle had been very busy spreading stories of the monsters and the huge red headed man in charge of them. He met De Menteith's first guard within seconds, cowering within the stair well, leading to the roof, to keep away from the Eagle flying overhead. He did not even know that Rory was behind him, until he tapped him on the shoulder. If he had had breeches on, instead of a kilt he would have soiled them, as he jumped into the air with fright. After he came down off the ceiling, he ran down the stairs and headed for the castle gate.

The next guard was braver and drew his sword, thinking he had an advantage over an unarmed man, no matter how big he was. A few seconds later and swordless, he too was running for the exit. Rory had easily disarmed him, as he lunged towards him with his sword aiming, for the middle of his body. The Hagpipe had been glowing hot since he had landed on Ben and it filled him with its power. Rory could move like lightning, and his hands were like iron as he snapped the man's sword in half, barehanded.

The bravest guards or those more scared of Laird John, guarded his chambers. All four of them fancied rushing at Rory all at once, which was a big mistake. They just got in one another's way and they were soon lying sprawled out on the ground on receipt of a tap from Rory's hand. Every sense in his body was on fire and the world around him moved in slow motion, as he cautiously opened the door to Laird John's chamber. As he had suspected, and his enhanced hearing had told him, he saw an empty room in front of him. The Laird hid behind the door with a drawn sword, ready to stab him in the back when he entered. Wooden doors in castles are made of very sturdy heavy wood as the Laird discovered, when it hit him in the face and knocked him out cold.

Rory picked him up by the scruff of the neck with one hand and carried him by his outstretched left arm like a rag doll on his walk down the stairs. By the time he reached the courtyard, the gate was open, and the draw-bridge was down, all done for him by the fleeing guards. No one wanted to stay and play with him, and he was quite disappointed at the lack of resistance. He still had not tested the power of the Hagpipe, and he relished a proper challenge.

Any resistance from any fleeing guards was short and swift when they met Rory's Dad with 'Hans' in his hands. They thought that they were seeing double and any brave enough to fight with a sword, soon had half a sword or no sword. The loyal Warriors of H.A.G.I within the castle just stood to the side, laughing at the rout of the guards. Ben decided that he did not want to be left out of the fun as he swooped down on the fleeing guards who are probably still running to this day.

Sir John De Menteith the younger had regained consciousness as Rory walked up to his Father, surrounded by his Warriors, who could not comprehend how easily they had regained the castle without loss of life. Rory dropped him to the ground in front of his Dad as Ben returned and hovered overhead. Ruaidri had conferred with Abbott MacCallum taking legal advice, prior to the campaign to retake the castle. He pulled a parchment from inside his sporran along with a quill and a corked bottle of ink.

There was no way that he was going to let this Menteith squirm out of any agreement using a legal loop hole. Ruaidri wanted confirmation that he could not make any future claim to his estate.

Sir John stood with his knees knocking and his nose bleeding before Ruaidri and all the witnesses, including some of own men, and literally under Eagle eyes. He looked up to the sky for some divine inspiration and salvation from God, but stared straight into the silent hovering eyes of Ben. He wore breeches and now he needed a clean pair. How can you fight someone who can control monsters, and with a trembling hand, he signed-over all of the Clan Mac Sween estates and the rights to them back to Ruaidri Mac Sween.

Sir John was put on the poorest horse in the stables with what personal possessions he could carry, and he was barred from ever setting foot on Mac Sween land again. He left to the jeers of the surrounding crowd. He had no intention of ever coming back to this cursed land, but the

Mac Sween's had just renewed a blood feud and gained another enemy!

Six warriors were despatched to escort the new Lady of Knapdale to her castle, as she sat in the back of her carriage, with the open wooden windows down, basking in the cheers of all present. Word was despatched to all the surrounding crofts, that the rightful ruler of Sween Castle had returned, and that he was holding a Christmas Party to end all parties to get reacquainted with his tenants.

The news spread that the monsters were there for the protection of the tenants of the estate, and that they had nothing to fear from them. Things would change now that the rightful Lord and Lady of Clan Mac Sween were back in charge of the land. They would all be better treated and more prosperous in the future.

It was Christmas Eve and those who could return to the castle and the adjacent Lochtown enjoyed the generous hospitality of the new Lord and Lady. Sween Castle was very well and richly supplied, and had a valuable personal stash hidden away by the previous corrupt and mean Laird John. The cache of the best beer, wine, brandy and whisky was cracked open and flowed freely, and all the recipients of it willingly took an oath of allegiance to their new master.

Rory pondered at the ease of this victory, unaware of the power and the allies being amassed by his stepdad John Grant, who had a new identity now as Evil Stan, and who was becoming stronger every day. If this growth in power continued, even the magical Hagpipe would be unable to stop Stan from enacting his revenge on Rory, and the inhuman plans that he had hatched against Rory's twin daughters.

For now, it was time to celebrate Christmas and this victory. The world still had to be saved and the Grail Box recovered, and Rory was still unaware that he was a father.

Things would work out, wouldn't they?

This story concludes in Book 3 Circles End.

J. A. Kay

Rory Mac Sween and the Secrets of Urquhart Castle

ISBN 978-3-99048-940-6
106 pages

Rory Mac Sween, eight years old and named after his missing father, is an intelligent and resilient boy. On finding the Hagpipe on his eighth birthday, Rory discovers strength beyond his years. The Hagpipe leads Rory on unimaginable adventures through time.